WHOA! I SPY A WEREWOLF

JUSTIN DAVIES
ILLUSTRATED BY KIM GEYER

ORCHARD

ORCHARD BOOKS

First published in Great Britain in 2020 by The Watts Publishing Group

1 3 5 7 9 10 8 6 4 2

Text copyright © Justin Davies 2020
Illustrations copyright © Kim Geyer 2020

A CIP catalogue record for this book is available from the British Library.

ISBN 978 1 40835 548 0

Printed and bound in Great Britain by
Clays Ltd, Elcograf S.p.A.

The paper and board used in this book are made from
wood from responsible sources

Orchard Books
An imprint of Hachette Children's Group
Part of The Watts Publishing Group Limited
Carmelite House, 50 Victoria Embankment, London EC4Y 0DZ

An Hachette UK Company
www.hachette.co.uk
www.hachettechildrens.co.uk

CONTENTS

1. NAILED IT!

'Whoa!'

Alice blinked twice, then looked at her splayed fingers again. Yep. This was a definite 'Whoa!' moment. Her fingernails had at least doubled in length since she'd clipped them yesterday. Maybe if she stared at them for long enough, she'd actually see them growing.

Looking up from her table, Alice glanced around Monsters' Munch. Apart from Doogie, the café owner, there were only a few people in the place. She decided she could risk a quick peek at her Ministry for Monsters welcome pack.

Alice had found the pack waiting for her downstairs

at Jobs4Monsters, her uncle Magnus's employment agency in Edinburgh. A lot had happened since her visit during the last school holiday, including being registered officially as a monster. She'd even had to provide a blood sample for the Ministry for Monsters database.

Alice placed one of the welcome pamphlets inside a menu in case anyone was watching. Monsters were good at keeping themselves hidden from prying eyes. They had to be. It was monster law.

Alice groaned at the pamphlet's terrible title: *So . . . You're Going to Be a Werewolf!* She flicked through, hoping there would be something in it about turbo-growth fingernails, but apart from a few basic sketches of 'The Six Stages of Werewolf Transformation' (which looked like they'd been drawn by a Year Two with their eyes shut) the pamphlet consisted entirely of a list of 'Don't's and 'Never's:

Ministry for Monsters

So... You're Going To Be
A Werewolf!

DON'T GO OUTSIDE TO LOOK AT A FULL MOON.

NEVER FORGET TO CARRY YOUR WEREWOLF
ANTIDOTE WITH YOU AT ALL TIMES.

DON'T PANIC IF YOU FORGET TO TAKE YOUR
ANTIDOTE...

**CALL THE MINISTRY IMMEDIATELY
FOR EMERGENCY CONTAINMENT.**

Alice didn't much like the sound of 'Emergency Containment'. It made her feel queasy just thinking about it.

She folded the pamphlet and dropped it into her satchel. 'Useless rubbish,' she muttered. What use was a list of things *not* to do? She already knew it was a crime to let yourself transform. Magnus had nearly got himself thrown into MonsterMax prison for forgetting to take his antidote during her last visit. What she *really* needed to know right now was if super-speed nail growth was normal for a Pre-T (pre-transformation werewolf) like her. Or if her hair was suddenly going to put on a hyper-growth spurt too, and start trailing along the ground behind her. Or maybe she'd begin howling without warning? Imagine doing that at the bus stop or during football practice! And what if she started craving chunks of raw meat, dripping with blood, instead of the divine-smelling chocolate orange muffins Doogie had been baking today?

Basically, she needed to know if having to cut her nails five times a week meant she was getting closer to her first transformation. The back of Alice's neck did the whole shiver-tingle thing. The idea terrified her, but it was also pretty cool. It would mean she was a proper monster, even if she had to take the werewolf antidote during a full moon. For ever.

Forget the Ministry, thought Alice. *Kiki will be able to help!*

She rummaged in her satchel and pulled out her new mini tablet, an early twelfth birthday present from her mum. Unlike her school friends, who were addicted to boring human sites, Alice had downloaded some weird and amazing monster apps. She turned the tablet on and clicked on ScreamScreen, a monster vlogging site she was obsessed with. By far the best monster vlogs on ScreamScreen were posted by Kiki.

Like all the most popular monsters on the monstanet, Kiki only used her first name. She was a cool young werewolf who'd started a vlog channel about what it was like growing up as a werewolf. She didn't spout useless Ministry rubbish. Instead she talked about properly important issues, like whether werewolves could be vegetarian (which Alice was), and the best ways to make the werewolf antidote taste better.

Alice selected a vlog and pressed play, quickly lowering the sound.

Kiki's face appeared, her beautiful eyes almost piercing the screen. All adult werewolves had eyes similar to a husky's, Alice had discovered. Kiki's eyes were an intense green, and Alice hoped she'd end up with something similar. She was a ginger after all.

Apart from Kiki's eyes, the thing Alice loved most of all was that Kiki looked and spoke like a regular person. But inside that regular person, she was dealing with all the rules and restrictions that came with being a werewolf. There was a lot of baggage to carry as a werewolf, and Kiki made it seem a lot less heavy. As she said at the end of every vlog:

"DON'T GET FREAKY, GET WITH KIKI!"

Alice did her best to remember those words every time she started to worry about the changes coming her way.

Amazingly, there was a chance that she would meet her new monster hero tomorrow. Kiki was hosting the Nessies – the monster world's annual awards show – and the whole team from Jobs4Monsters had been invited. Even *more* amazingly, Alice had been nominated in the 'Bravest Monster' category for helping to rescue the royal cyclops. If she won, Kiki would present her with the award! Alice's neck tingled again. But this time, it was sheer excitement.

A sudden shadow loomed over her. Alice instantly slammed the tablet face-down on the table.

'Thought you'd like another Steamo Creamo Peanutccino,' said Doogie, placing a mug on the table. 'You guzzled the last one faster than a vampire in a blood bank.'

A mouth-watering waft of chocolate and peanut butter drifted up from the mug. If she wasn't mistaken, Doogie had added a pinch of cinnamon.

'What?' she stammered. 'Oh, yeah. Thank you. It was delicious.'

Alice could feel her face turning red as she looked up at the faun. Doogie's bushy eyebrows had joined together in a hairy caterpillar frown. Yep. He'd seen what she'd been watching.

'Sorry, Doogie,' she said. 'I know I'm not supposed to watch this stuff here.'

Doogie smiled. 'Be careful. There's a reason I wear this beanie over my faun horns, you know. A lot of my customers are human.' He leaned in to whisper, 'And there's a boy over there who's been watching you.'

Alice peered round Doogie. All she could see was a mass of curly black hair hiding behind a magazine. 'Are you sure?' she said.

Doogie smirked. 'Quite sure. Maybe he fancies you.'

Alice rolled her eyes. 'Don't you start,' she said. 'Miss Pinky's desperate to set me up with someone.

Ever since you got together with my uncle, she's had nobody to matchmake.'

The faun flipped Alice's tablet over. 'Ah-ha!' he whispered. 'The star herself. What do you think she'll be wearing? Something super-glamorous and ultra-fabulous?'

Alice laughed. She reckoned Kiki would try to keep it real for her legions of fans. Alice had decided to keep it real too, by point-blank refusing to wear a dress or skirt. Instead she'd allowed Miss Pinky – Jobs4Monsters' newly-promoted Deputy Manager – to pick out a sparkly hoodie and gold sneakers for her when they'd gone outfit shopping earlier in the week.

Doogie's eyes gleamed. 'Maybe just wait until you're back in the office to catch up on the monster vlogs. OK?'

Alice nodded sheepishly. 'No problem. Oh, and the cinnamon is a nice touch.'

'Only your super smellability could pick up on that, Alice! It was just the tiniest amount.' Doogie winked and headed back to the counter.

Alice bent down to put the tablet in her satchel. As she pulled herself back up, another shadow fell over the table.

'*Excusez-moi!* May I sit 'ere?'

The boy's face was framed by a crazy amount of curly black hair. In one hand he held a mug topped with whipped cream, while the other held one of Doogie's muffins. A cherry and berry one, Alice decided after a quick sniff.

He placed his mug and muffin on Alice's table and dragged the other chair out, swinging into it with so much energy that his curls bounced around his head like coiled springs. Then he grinned, revealing a gap between his front teeth, before biting into his muffin.

'*Miam*! This is *délicieux!*' The boy's eyes shone in

11

the sunlight streaming in from outside. Alice noticed they were brown, flecked with orange. 'Do you think there are really *des monstres* in this café?' he asked, mouth half-stuffed with muffin.

'W . . . what?'

'Monsters,' said the boy. 'Are there real monsters in this café?'

Alice's head spun like a Waltzer at the fairground. 'What do you mean?'

The boy's grin widened. 'It is called Monsters' Moonch, yes?'

Hearing 'munch' pronounced like that would normally have had Alice in stitches, but not right now. Right now, she didn't know what to say or think. And if she wasn't mistaken, the boy was trying to peer inside her satchel.

She scraped her chair back and stood up, clutching her satchel tightly to her chest. 'Of course there aren't

12

any monsters,' she said. 'They don't exist.' She tried to smile. 'Sorry, I have to go.'

'But what about your *chocolat chaud*?' said the boy, pointing to her mug.

'You can have it,' shouted Alice as she hurried away.

2. SECURITY ➡

CLEARANCE LEVEL ONE

Alice dashed to the end of the street and turned into the narrow alleyway which ran along between the rows of old houses. She paused for a moment to catch her breath. That annoying boy had ruined her morning. She'd been quite content, breathing in the hundreds of heavenly scents of Doogie's café and getting excited about seeing Kiki in person at the Nessies. And then he'd butted in with his bouncy-haired head.

What if he'd caught a bit of Kiki's vlog?

Her tummy twisted like a tightly coiled rope. She could get into big trouble for this.

Alice carried on down the alleyway, almost tripping

up over a discarded can as she reached the back entrance to Jobs4Monsters. The front door was off-limits after Magnus had instigated bizarre new security measures to deal with a sudden increase in office visitors. Measures which everyone, including staff and family, had to comply with.

An industrial-sized, metal wheelie bin now stood in the pokey, weed-covered yard by the back door. Alice approached it and thumped the top.

'Oi!' she whispered into a small hole drilled into the side. 'Let me in.'

A deep grunt reverberated from within the bin, followed by an equally deep and gravelly voice. 'Name the current minister for monsters,' it said.

'There isn't one,' replied Alice.

'Why's that?' asked the voice.

'Because the last one was turned to stone by Medusa,' said Alice, shivering at the memory of how her Gorgon friend had accidentally petrified Gideon Dragstorm, the evil former Minister for Monsters.

'Correct answer,' said the voice. The lid sprang open and a large head, totally covered in chocolate brown hair, appeared over the edge.

'Thank you for using
SASQUATCH SECURITY SERVICES.
Don't botch it . . . let the sasquatch watch it!'

The monster reached out and unlocked the door.

'Thank you, Ronald,' Alice said, smiling at the creature. 'Although you should probably ask a different question next time. That's the third time you've asked me that one.'

The sasquatch smiled back, revealing a mouth crammed with stumpy yellow teeth. Making a mental note to bring him a toothbrush next time, Alice made her way down the corridor to the office.

She was greeted by a cacophony of grunts, roars and screams. An overpowering stench of sweaty-furred and sticky-feathered monsters reminded her that a werewolf's super-powered sense of smell wasn't always an advantage. Waving her hand in front of her nose, she peered into the crowded reception room.

'Alice!' cried Magnus from behind a boisterous crowd of short, bearded, green-clothed creatures. He pushed his way through the throng. His ginger hair was in its usual dishevelled state. 'Where have you been?'

'Sorry,' said Alice. 'I stayed for a second mug.'

Magnus rolled his eyes. 'You must have gone through the entire menu by now.'

'Almost,' admitted Alice. 'Who are they?' she added, raising her voice as the green-clothed creatures broke into song. It might have been pleasant to listen to, only they'd all picked either a different tune, or completely different words.

'Leprechauns,' shouted Magnus. 'And I'd like you to deal with them, please. I've got a video interview with a krakagon in a minute.' He put a hand on his forehead. 'See if you can shut them up, Alice. My head is still killing me.'

Earlier in the week, Magnus had travelled to the mountains to interview a stone giant for a quarry excavating job. He'd stood on a rock to shout up at the creature, and the stone giant, being a) short-sighted, and b) stupid, had picked up Magnus's rock for a snack. Magnus said he'd only missed being ground to a pulp by the giant's teeth by jumping to safety. Unfortunately he had landed on his head.

Now *definitely* wasn't the time for Alice to tell him that she might have allowed a human to see a bit of the monster world. She just had to hope that boy wouldn't come looking for her.

'What am I doing with these leprechauns then?' she asked, looking at the gaggle of rowdy creatures.

'Check they're genuine, will you?' said Magnus. 'Nobody wants to hire a leprechaun who makes porridge instead of rainbows.'

Alice spent the next ten minutes putting the leprechauns through their paces. By the time she'd finished, half had been sent packing. At least two turned out to be lady goblins wearing false beards. They'd come to Jobs4Monsters hoping no-one would notice they'd brought ordinary saucepans with them instead of magical leprechaun pots.

'Phew!' exclaimed Miss Pinky, emerging from her new Deputy Manager's office just as Alice closed the door on the grumbling goblins. 'Am I glad that's over!'

'What have you been up to?' asked Alice.

'Well,' said Miss Pinky, running her fingers along her white whiskers. 'I've been trying to find a replacement tooth fairy for a dental practice. The last one was swallowed by a minotaur during an extraction, and now no-one seems interested in the job. And before that my friend Jeanie called. She's the chief experimental chemist at MonLab and she's looking for a new assistant.'

'What's MonLab?'

'It stands for Monster Laboratory,' explained Miss Pinky. 'They make medicines for the monster community. It's where you'll be getting your werewolf antidote from someday.'

Alice smiled at her friend. It was obvious Miss Pinky was enjoying her new position. She'd been the Jobs4Monsters receptionist, but since helping Alice to rescue the cyclops, Magnus had promoted her. And nobody deserved it more than Miss Pinky. Alice was proud to call the half mermaid, half giant cat monster her best mate.

Maybe I should tell her about the boy, she thought.

Alice opened her mouth to speak, but Miss Pinky suddenly threw her against the wall.

'Incoming!' she screamed, as a blue-grey blur rushed by. 'I wish he wouldn't do that,' she spluttered in the swirling cloud. 'Dustin's supposed to *collect* the dust, not create it.'

Alice rubbed her eyes. Jobs4Monsters had taken on a house brownie to keep the place clean who was forever zipping through, rotating like a car-wash brush. Occasionally Dustin would stop for a moment to pick

21

out some dust from his straggly hair. Alice wasn't sure if it was hair from his head, body or face, as the brownie was sheathed in hair from top to bottom with just his pink toes sticking out.

She quickly closed her eyes as the brownie whirled past again. For a creature who only came up to Alice's chest, Dustin still managed to cause chaos. 'I think he's actually making things worse,' she said, brushing a layer of dust off her top.

Miss Pinky licked her whiskers clean. 'You try telling a brownie how to do their job.'

Magnus opened his office door. 'Ah, Miss Pinky,' he said. 'I don't suppose you found that krakagon translation app? I can't tell if this one is saying he wants to work for us, or eat me for his dinner.'

'These krakagons are new to me,' said Alice, scribbling it down in her notebook. 'Are they a sort of splicer too?'

'Yes,' said Miss Pinky. 'Although us splicers aren't called that any more.'

'You're not?' asked Alice, looking up from her notebook.

Miss Pinky laughed. 'Didn't I tell you I was a MOM now?'

Alice stared at Miss Pinky, confused. 'You're a . . . mum?' An image popped into her mind of Miss Pinky trundling a litter of merma-kittens around in a pram.

'No!' Miss Pinky hooted with laughter. 'A MOM. A Mixed Origin Monster. The Ministry thinks it's more respectful.'

'I didn't think there was anyone running the Ministry right now,' said Alice.

'There isn't,' said Magnus. 'But that doesn't stop the pencil pushers who work there from issuing orders.' He sighed. 'I'd better see if I can make myself understood to *This* MOM!'

As soon as he'd closed his office door, Alice turned to Miss Pinky. 'I think I might have messed up,' she said, quickly explaining about the boy.

'This calls for an EBB!' said Miss Pinky, grabbing her by the arm.

'A what?'

'Emergency Bog Briefing,' said Miss Pinky, leading Alice into the washroom. She selected one of the stalls, pulled Alice in and locked the door.

'Right,' said Miss Pinky. 'Out with it.'

'No, keep it in,' said a watery-sounding voice from somewhere inside the toilet. 'I've only just got back after that hairball of a cleaner flushed me away.'

A curling wisp of green mist rose up out of the toilet, transforming into the familiar outline of Fergus Fingal, the poltergeist Jobs4Monsters had acquired during Alice's last visit. He hovered in the air with a mischievous grin on his face.

'Have you been naughty, Alice?' he asked.

'I don't know,' began Alice. 'The thing is, I sort of—'

But she was interrupted again, this time by Miss Pinky's phone trilling an alert.

'Hold it!'

cried Miss Pinky, as she swiped her phone screen frantically.

'Yes, do please keep holding it,' said Fergus with a giggle. 'Or at least use a different loo.'

'Wow!' screamed Miss Pinky, so loudly that Fergus exploded into a fine vapour. 'No way! Epic!'

Alice craned her neck to see Miss Pinky's phone. '*Strictly Monstering*,' she read off the screen. She looked at Miss Pinky, raising her eyebrow. 'I thought my uncle said you weren't to look at gossip sites during office hours.'

Miss Pinky pouted. 'I'm on a toilet break. And anyway, this is big news!'

Fergus reappeared under the door and turned a somersault in the air. 'Come on then! Dish it!'

'It's Kiki,' said Miss Pinky, jumping from paw to paw as if she really did need the toilet. 'She's here. In Edinburgh. Right now. For a pre-Nessies press conference.'

'What? Where? When?' yelled Alice, grabbing the phone and eagerly reading the screen. She couldn't believe her hero was so close, but she still had to wait a whole day to see her.

Miss Pinky reached through Fergus and unbolted the door for Alice. 'Come on,' she said, eyes twinkling and whiskers twitching like a sea urchin feeling around for its supper. 'Why are we bogging around in this bog, when we could be blagging our way into that press conference?'

'But we aren't journalists,' said Alice, starting to wash her hands before remembering she hadn't actually been for a wee.

'Alice MacAlister!' exclaimed Miss Pinky. 'I'm surprised at you! You're up for the Bravest Monster award for breaking into Gideon Dragstorm's ghoul-ridden fortress, saving a cyclops and surviving death-by-kraken. If anyone can sneak into this press conference, you can.'

Alice thought about this for a second. 'You're right,' she said.

'I know,' said Miss Pinky. 'So come on! There are two new reporters in town and they've got some very important questions to ask.'

3. SECURITY ➠
CLEARANCE LEVEL TWO

Less than half an hour after leaving the office, Alice and Miss Pinky were stumbling over a stony wasteland in an abandoned dockyard, surrounded by rusting old boat sheds.

'Are you sure this is the place?' asked Alice, stepping carefully around an especially prickly-looking thistle.

'Absolutely,' replied Miss Pinky, springing over a crumbling section of wall.

Alice clambered over the wall after her, snagging her satchel on an old brick. Sometimes, she thought, having Miss Pinky's cat-like leaping skills would be a distinct advantage.

She paused to read a sign saying:

DANGER — KEEP OUT.

'That's the third warning notice I've seen,' she said, staring up at a massive concrete tower looming above them. 'I don't like it here.'

'Chill!' said Miss Pinky. 'My sources are never wrong.'

Alice surveyed the crumbling concrete and mangled bits of metal littering the ground. 'I think this might be an exception,' she said, looking at Miss Pinky. 'And you can probably take that off now.'

Miss Pinky pulled off the surgical mask she'd worn to cover her whiskers. They'd taken the bus to get down to the docks and although most humans just thought Miss Pinky was a bit alternative and wore stuck-on whiskers as a fashion statement, it was usually easier to pretend she was suffering from a terrible cold. Alice had seen two tourists wearing similar masks from the bus.

'Yuck!' Alice pinched her nose. 'I could do with a mask myself. This place stinks like fermented fish fingers. Why would anyone hold a press conference here?'

'Because,' said Miss Pinky, making a beeline for the tower, 'there'll be tons of monsters around, so they need to take monster-sized precautions.'

'Like hold press conferences in about-to-collapse towers?'

'Exactly,' said Miss Pinky, holding up a fist to knock on the door.

'Hold on!' Alice stepped in front of her and gave the door a quick sniff. There was a gut-churning mix of smells, including one which Alice instantly recognised: werewolf. 'You were right,' she said. 'This is definitely the place.'

'Told you so!' cried Miss Pinky. She thumped the door, then rummaged in her bag, pulling out what looked to Alice like a gym membership card. She then unscrewed a bright red lipstick and scribbled **PRESS** across the card. 'Might as well try and look the part!'

A muffled shuffling and grunting came from the other side of the door. 'State your purpose!' boomed a deep, gravelly voice.

'We're very important, award-winning journalists,' said Miss Pinky, winking at Alice.

A hatch in the door flipped open, revealing a rectangle of dark brown knotted fur and a large pair of green eyes. A whiff of damp wool and pine trees wafted out. 'ID please,' ordered the voice.

Miss Pinky held up her fake press pass. The green eyes scanned it, then the hatch slammed shut.

'Oh dear,' whispered Alice. 'He didn't buy it.'

But then the door creaked open. Alice gasped as a furry, frisbee-sized hand shot from the gloom and beckoned them in with a fat, hairy finger.

Once inside, Alice's eyes quickly adjusted to the dark interior, revealing a bear-like monster with straggly mud-coloured hair. Dangleberries hung like baubles from his long arms, and yellowy, twisted nails grew from weirdly long toes. The creature's face reminded Alice of Ronald back at Jobs4Monsters.

'Are you a sasquatch?' Alice blurted out, instantly realising this might sound rude.

'Certainly not!' said the monster, with a slight American twang. 'I'm a Big Foot. The name's Brian.'

'But you are a security guard?' asked Alice.

'You got it!' said Brian. **'"You need a Big Foot to kick out Big Problems!"'**

Miss Pinky laughed. 'That's very good. Did you just make that up?'

'No,' said Brian. 'It's my motto. There's a ton of competition in the monster security industry, so you need a catchy slogan to stay ahead of the game.'

The Big Foot looked down at Alice. 'Where is your press pass?'

Miss Pinky pushed Alice forward. 'She's with me, Brian. Alice is my apprentice reporter.'

Alice dutifully pulled her notepad and pen from her satchel. 'We're from *Strictly Monstering*,' she said. 'Because monster gossip won't report itself!'

Brian let out a deep, throaty laugh, blasting Alice with a not-very-pleasant odour of chewed meat. 'You have a motto too!' Then he directed them to a door on the other side of the room. 'It's about to start,' he said. 'You're just in time.'

They hurried over and pushed the door open. Immediately they found themselves sucked into a throng of bodies, some human-like, others most definitely not. Alice brushed past a couple of goblin-like creatures, one hefting a camera almost as big as herself on to her shoulder.

'They're from GNN,' explained Miss Pinky. 'Goblin News Network.'

'OK,' said Alice, shivering suddenly as if she'd just walked through an ice curtain.

'And that ghost who just flew through you is from GNN,' Miss Pinky added.

'A ghost works at Goblin News?'

'No, silly,' said Miss Pinky. 'Ghost News Network.'

'And I suppose that giant over there works for GNN as well,' guessed Alice. 'Giant News Network?'

'That would just be confusing,' said Miss Pinky. 'She's a reporter with GBUK. Giant Broadcasting UK.'

'Right,' said Alice, shaking her head. She turned to look at the stage, where a table with microphones had been set up. 'Crikey! And what's that thing up there?'

She pointed to a truly grotesque monster with gigantic lion's paws, green bat-like wings, and a pointed scorpion tail which snapped overhead. Its human face

35

scowled out at everyone from under a mane of greasy black hair.

'Wow!' Miss Pinky stared at the creature. 'A manticore. I did not expect to see one of them here.'

A manticore! Alice remembered reading about these creatures in *The Official Monster Guide*. The *OMG* listed them as a category six, the highest danger rating possible. She was just about to

ask Miss Pinky what such a dangerous monster was doing at Kiki's press conference when she got another shock. Through the crowd she'd just caught a glimpse of the boy from the café. He was looking directly at her.

What was HE doing here?

Alice was so surprised to see him – and he still had that wide, tooth-gap smile on his face – that she totally missed the star attraction walking on to the stage. It took a dig in the side from Miss Pinky to alert her to the action.

'If you could take your eyes off that boy for a moment,' yelled Miss Pinky over the applause, 'the reason we've just gate-crashed this press conference is here.'

'What?' Alice stammered. 'Oh. Yeah. Right.'

She turned back to the stage. The boy would have to wait. Alice wasn't going to let him distract her from this moment. Although trying to catch a glimpse of Kiki through the heaving mob of feathered, furred and wart-covered monsters was proving impossible.

Time to make a move.

Alice ducked into a gap between the camera-wielding goblin and the giant reporter. She wove her way towards the stage, dodging a wing here and a spiked tail there, and narrowly avoided slipping in a steaming pile of centaur manure. She'd almost made it to the front of the crowd when a roar ripped around the room, making the floor vibrate and dust fall from the ceiling.

'Silence!'

As she forced herself between two men with large gills in their necks, who were giving off the sort of smell normally found in the tropical fish section of the garden centre, Alice saw the red-faced, snarling manticore. Its scorpion tail clacked over the crowd. Then it scuttered sideways, revealing a figure standing on a podium.

It was Kiki. And she was staring right at Alice!

4. FREAK OUT!

Kiki's eyes weren't green after all. In fact, Alice couldn't really tell what colour they were because cameras were flashing all over the place. When the flashes calmed down a bit, she saw that they were an unusual grey-yellow, a colour Alice had never seen on a werewolf before.

As the star looked out over the assembled journalists and reporters, Alice couldn't help feeling a bit deflated. For some reason, she hadn't expected Kiki to wear fake contact lenses for her vlog. It wasn't exactly keeping it real.

'Good morning, adoring fans,' announced Kiki into

a microphone, sending her smooth and rather dramatic voice rolling around the room. It was nothing like the chatty friends-just-chilling voice Alice was used to.

Applause broke out, giving Alice the chance to take in the vision on the stage. Glittering jewels sparkled from Kiki's neck and ears. She wore a long, shimmering dress covered in silvery-blue sequins, while her hair was twisted into an elaborate sculpture, pierced by what looked like solid silver – and very sharp – chopsticks. Miss Pinky would be guaranteed to try and replicate the look by the end of the day.

'She scrubs up well,' said one of the fish-gill reporters standing next to Alice as he scribbled frantically in his notebook.

'Imagine what she'll be wearing tomorrow night!' said the other, holding his phone up to take a photo.

As the applause died away, Kiki spoke again. 'What an honour it must be to have me host this year's

Nessie awards.' She paused, gazing around the room, then clicked her fingers in the manticore's direction.

'Clap!' roared the creature, cracking his tail like a whip. With the ghastly manticore's angry eyes glaring out at the crowd, Alice felt she had no option, and began clapping along with everyone else.

'At tomorrow night's ceremony,' continued Kiki, 'we shall reveal the best of all monsters, and history will indeed be made.' She clicked her fingers and everyone clapped again. Alice didn't really feel like joining in, but she spotted the manticore's scorpion tail lashing around, and clapped until her hands stung.

Kiki then began to take questions, pointing first to the gill-necked reporter. Alice spotted glimmering blue-green scales poking out above his collar. *He must be part merman*, she thought.

'Right . . . yes . . . thank you, Kiki,' said the reporter, fumbling with his notebook. 'I'm from FishnetFlix. Can you tell us what you'll be wearing at the Nessies?'

Kiki smiled, her teeth gleaming white against her glittering blue-painted lips. 'Good question,' she said. 'Maybe your mermaid scales. Next!'

Alice winced. If Kiki had been trying to raise a laugh with her joke, she hadn't come close. Judging by the reporter's stony face, he didn't think it was funny either.

Alice fought her way back to Miss Pinky, feeling a little bit confused by what she'd just seen and heard. As she did, she walked straight into the boy from the café.

'*Excusez-moi!*' he said. 'I am sorry.'

Alice gasped and clutched her chest. 'What are you doing here?' she hissed.

He smiled and whistled through the gap in his teeth. 'It's funny,' he said. 'You are surprised to see me 'ere, but I am not surprised to see you.'

The orange flecks in his eyes still flared brightly, like they had in the café. But now that Alice really looked at them, she realised they had the piercing intensity found in a husky's eyes. The boy was a werewolf too! She was sure of it. A quick sniff confirmed it.

'Did you just smell me?' asked the boy.

'Might have,' said Alice, recovering. 'So why aren't you surprised to see me here?'

The boy laughed. 'Because I knew you were *un loup-garou* just like *moi*!'

'A what?'

'A werewolf,' said the boy. 'In France, we are called *loup-garou*.'

Alice sniffed him again, this time pulling a face. Boy werewolves had similar personal hygiene issues to human boys. 'Go on then, *monsieur* detective. How did you know?'

The boy held up three fingers. 'First, your eyes are

44

the eyes of a werewolf. Second, you were, I think, watching this Kiki. And third,' he said triumphantly, 'I heard everything the café owner said to you.'

Alice glared at him. 'How?'

The boy shrugged. 'I cannot help it,' he said. 'I can hear a mouse two rooms away.'

Makes sense, thought Alice. Magnus had super-hearing too. All werewolves had one heightened sense.

'It's rude to listen to a private conversation,' said Alice.

'But, he was correct, the man in the café,' said the boy. 'You must take more care in front of humans.'

The boy pronounced 'humans' as 'oomuns', which made Alice want to burst into laughter, She forced herself not to. They stared at each other, then both stuck their hands out at exactly the same moment. This time Alice did laugh. They both did.

'I'm Alice.'

'Louis,' said the boy. 'And now I hope we are *amis* – friends.'

Alice smiled at Louis. He smiled back with an even wider smile than before.

'There you are, Alice!' Miss Pinky jostled her way through the crowd, sending a couple of scowling fairy journalists fluttering up into the air. 'Are you going to introduce me to your new friend?'

'This is Louis,' said Alice. 'The boy I told you about from the café. He's a werewolf.'

'That's just as well,' said Miss Pinky, winking at Alice. Then she shook Louis's hand. 'What are you doing at this press conference?'

'I wanted to see this Kiki,' said Louis.

'So you sneaked in too!' said Alice, laughing.

Louis shook his head, making his curls bounce. 'I am supposed to be here. I came with my mother. She is a special guest at these Nessie awards.'

'Really?' Alice said. Louis was becoming more intriguing by the second.

'*Oui*. She is Lucille Loup-Garou. The French *Ministre des Monstres*. She is the international guest of honour at the Nessies.'

'Wow, wow, wow!' exclaimed Miss Pinky. 'You're one of the Loup-Garous!' She looked at Alice. 'They're like a werewolf dynasty in France. Almost monster royalty.'

'There's *ma mère*,' said Louis, 'talking to that reporter.'

Alice followed Louis' finger to where a tall woman was giving an interview. The woman looked at Alice for a moment and nodded her head ever so slightly. Even from a distance, Alice could make out the flame-orange specks in Lucille Loup-Garou's eyes, but against her darker skin, they seemed to glow even brighter than Louis's. Something about her height and elegant posture reminded Alice of Medusa, and she felt a sudden twinge of sadness that the gorgon and her cyclops husband weren't going to be at the Nessies. They were on an extended holiday in Greece, catching up with old friends. Probably very old, considering they had both been around for over two thousand years.

'So the Loup-Garous are famous in France?' asked Alice.

'In monster circles they are,' said Miss Pinky. 'I mean, Loup-Garou even *means* werewolf, doesn't it, Louis?'

Louis nodded.

'Wait a minute,' said Alice. 'So, you're a werewolf and your name is Louis Werewolf?'

Louis dipped his head and looked up at Alice through his bouncing curls. 'Ah . . . *oui*. Yes. I suppose it does.'

Alice laughed. 'I love it!'

Miss Pinky meanwhile was checking her phone. 'This

is so exciting!' she squealed. 'The press conference is all over *Strictly Monstering*! They're already calling Kiki a diva.'

'She was acting a bit diva-ish,' said Alice. 'Not at all what I was expecting. Maybe she's more normal one-on-one.'

'Why don't you find out?' suggested Miss Pinky. 'Go and see if you can speak to her before she leaves.'

Alice's tummy flipped over. 'Really?'

Louis grabbed her arm. '*Bon idée!* Great idea! *Allez!*' he shouted. 'Come on! We go together to meet *la diva!*'

The crowd was thinning out by the time they made it back to the stage. Hesitating by the steps, Alice watched as the manticore unleashed its curled-up tail and aimed its gleaming sting at an airborne pixie who was pointing a ridiculously long zoom lens at Kiki.

'I've changed my mind,' she said. 'That thing looks lethal.'

On cue, the monster swiped at the pixie with a clawed foot. Its talons gleamed like freshly sharpened chef's knives.

'Pah!' exclaimed Louis. 'It is probably all show and no sting.'

'*Probably?*' Alice ducked as the scorpion tail snapped over their heads. But Louis, it seemed, was already half way up the stairs. She had a feeling he was showing off.

'Halt!' roared the manticore. 'Or I will sting you and throw your bodies to my nest of hungry infants.'

'*Non*!' said Louis. 'You will not. This would be in contravention of the international treaty on the use of powers against underage monsters.'

The manticore curled back its tail. Alice used his

moment of confusion to join Louis onstage. 'Is that an actual thing?' she whispered.

'I don't know,' Louis whispered back. 'My *maman* talks about stuff like this all the time.'

They hurried across the stage. Kiki whipped around, her sequin dress sparkling magnificently.

'Little fanlings!' she cooed in her deep, smooth voice. 'How perfect! Did Barbie let you through my security cordon?'

'Barbie?' Alice looked back at the manticore, who was glaring at them.

'It's short for Barbarus,' he growled through gritted teeth.

'Well, never mind,' said Kiki. 'Come this way.' She pointed to a spot about five metres away from her. 'Stand there and don't slouch.'

Alice straightened her shoulders. Kiki was nothing like she'd imagined her to be when watching her vlog.

Maybe this is how she really is, she thought. It was entirely possible that the online Kiki was just an act. Her mum was always saying that you couldn't trust anything you saw online. *Looks like Mum was right. Again*.

'What can I do for you?' asked Kiki, tapping her foot impatiently.

Alice remained silent, until she felt a sharp nudge in her side from Louis.

'Say something,' he whispered.

She took a breath, trembling slightly. A barrage of scents hit her suddenly. There were so many, it was impossible to name even one. It was like stepping on to a massive bus rammed with people and breathing in all their odours at once. Nerves were obviously getting the better of her. *Get a grip*! she told herself.

'It's . . . um . . . great to meet you?' said Alice. It came out more like a question.

'Of course it is,' said Kiki, matter-of-factly.

'And . . . er . . . I love watching your vlogs,' continued Alice. 'You always give such good advice.'

'Such as?'

Alice racked her brain. 'Well, like how you say that bravery comes from within, whether facing school exams or your first werewolf transformation.'

'I said that?'

'Yes,' replied Alice. 'I always remember it because it's the sort of thing my friend Medusa would say.'

This had an instant effect on Kiki. 'You are friends with Medusa?' she asked, stepping closer.

Alice nodded.

'Name?' snapped Kiki. 'Tell me your name!'

Alice flinched, fighting an urge to back away. 'Alice. Alice MacAlister.'

Kiki was silent for a moment. Then her face switched into an instant smile, flashing icy-white teeth.

'Well, well. If it isn't the famous Alice MacAlister.'

'You are famous?' whispered Louis.

'Of course she is famous!' Kiki took another step closer. 'She is nominated for the Bravest Monster Nessie! She is the courageous hero who defeated Gideon Dragstorm and rescued the cyclops from the jaws of a kraken!'

'*Zut alors!*' Louis gazed at Alice with an astonished look on his face. 'That was you?'

Alice glared at him. 'There's no reason to sound so surprised. Although I wasn't on my own. And the kraken was never going to eat anyone.'

'This *is* exciting,' said Kiki, pushing Louis to the side. 'To be in the presence of such greatness.'

Alice pulled a *who, me?* face. 'Hardly.'

Kiki tutted. 'Never underestimate yourself,' she said.

Finally, thought Alice. *The sort of advice you'd expect from Kiki.*

'I never do,' Kiki added. She stepped even closer.

'Let me shake the hand of the brave Alice MacAlister.'

'Oh, I wouldn't go that far—'

Kiki lunged forward and grabbed both her hands. Alice felt an instant surge within her. She'd heard about sudden rushes of blood to the head, but this was more of a sudden rush *from* the head. And legs. And arms. When she tried to pull away, she discovered Kiki's hands were locked on to hers like magnets.

As she began to sway and stars flashed in front of her eyes, she was suddenly pulled back. Her hands ripped apart from Kiki's, her fingers tingling as if hit by a bolt of electricity.

'What did you do that for, boy?' snapped Kiki, as Alice tried to get her breath back.

'*Pardonnez-moi*,' said Louis. 'But Alice did not seem very well.'

'What was that?' asked Alice, still swaying slightly. She held on to Louis's shoulder to steady herself.

'Oh . . . probably my electric personality,' said Kiki. 'I have that effect on other monsters.'

She stared at Alice. Despite the stars still floating around in front of her, Alice could have sworn Kiki's eyes were now a light shade of blue. What sort of werewolf *was* she?

'I suggest you take your friend out for some fresh air,' said Kiki, dismissing them both with a flick of her hand. 'Her skin has taken on the pallor of yesterday's porridge.'

With that she stalked off the stage, with Barbie scurrying after her.

5. FRENCH REVELATION

The next few minutes passed in a foggy blur. They were outside, she knew that much. Alice hadn't felt this weak since she'd mistakenly entered the school sports day cross-country race instead of the country dancing. She'd needed a lie-down and half a pack of jelly babies to recover from that.

'Here, have some water.' A bottle was pressed into her hand. '*Allez-y*. Drink.'

Alice gulped and gulped. **Wow!** She was thirsty. She rubbed her eyes and looked up at Louis.

'What did Kiki do to me?' She held up her hands and examined them. They looked normal, no burn marks or anything. Alice gulped some more water, beginning to feel more like herself again. 'Do you think Kiki's a MOM? You know, a splicer?'

'*Peut-être,*' said Louis. 'It is possible. Like a werewitch, you mean?'

'Is there such a thing?'

Louis nodded. 'There are also **werewizards** and **werefairies** and **weregiants.**'

Alice felt a surge of anger. 'Well if she is, I think she should have told her fans.'

As she got to her feet, she spotted Miss Pinky skipping out of the building with Louis's mum behind her.

'Look at you, all starstruck and fainting away!' shrieked Miss Pinky, grabbing Alice's hands. 'I know I can get carried away at an M-Pop gig, but even I've never been carried out before!'

Alice shook her hands free. Her fingers were still

aching from Kiki's strong grasp. She massaged them for a second.

'Sorry,' said Miss Pinky. 'I just wanted to touch the hands that held Kiki's. How was it? What did you guys talk about?'

Alice looked at Miss Pinky. She'd gone to so much effort to get them into the press conference, it seemed a bit ungrateful to moan about it.

'You know,' she said. 'This and that. She did seem quite pleased to meet me.'

'Told you she would be!' Miss Pinky beamed. 'You're up for an award! Of course she wanted to meet you.'

Alice tried her best to smile. 'She's not quite what I expected.'

Miss Pinky laughed knowingly. 'Big stars never are!'

'*Alors, Mademoiselle* Pinky,' said Louis's mum, stepping forward. 'Are you going to introduce me?'

'Soz!' Miss Pinky slapped her head. 'Totally forgot

my manners. Madame Loup-Garou, this is my bestie, Alice. Alice, this is Madame Loup-Garou, the French Minister for Monsters.'

'Please,' said the Minister. 'Call me Lucille.'

Alice shook her hand. After Kiki's lightning touch, Lucille's hands felt warm and soft.

'It's lovely to meet you,' said Alice, wondering if she should curtsey.

'I see you have met my son,' said Lucille, rubbing Louis's head. His hair sprang right back into place. 'It is wonderful that he has made a friend here in Edinburgh. You will perhaps show him the sights?'

Alice looked at Louis. 'Do you want to see the city?'

Louis's eyes gleamed. '*Oui!* I would love to! So far, I have only been to a café.' He winked at Alice. 'Although that was *très* interesting!'

'Perfect,' said Lucille, smiling broadly. 'It is better that he does not explore alone.' She leaned in to whisper in Alice's ear. 'Louis does not often mix with humans, but with an expert, he will be OK.'

'Am I an expert?' said Alice.

Lucille nodded. 'Mademoiselle Pinky tells me you are new to our monster world.'

'I suppose I am.'

'*Bien*. Then you are his guide to all things human.'

'And Louis is bound to know tons about werewolving,' said Miss Pinky. She smiled at Alice. 'It's great to see you've made another monster friend.' Then she looked worried. 'But I'll still be your bestie, won't I?'

Alice laughed. 'Of course!'

Having walked to the bus stop and waited for ages for a bus to turn up, Alice and Louis were finally on their way into the city.

'Louis, will you stop doing that?' Alice said. 'You'll get us into trouble.' She looked around the top deck of the bus. The other passengers were glaring at them.

'*Quoi*?' said Louis.

Alice pulled his hand away from the 'stop' button. 'Don't keep ringing the bell,' she said. 'You're making the bus stop for no reason.' She threw him a 'be sensible' sort of look, but it ended up as a smile. 'Have you really never been on a bus before?'

Louis shook his head, hair bouncing, eyes gleaming. 'We live at the *Résidence*, which is in the middle of the countryside. In France,' he explained in a low voice, 'the monsters do not live so close to the humans.'

Alice suddenly reached for the bell and pressed it. 'This *is* our stop!' She grabbed Louis and they hurtled down the stairs and out on to the crowded pavement.

Unlike on the bus, Louis didn't seem to realise there was a button to press in order to cross the road. After saving him on two pedestrian crossings, Alice decided it would be fun to watch some of the street entertainers performing. Louis was especially fascinated by the human statues who covered themselves in metallic paint, only moving when someone threw a coin into their pot.

'You must have these in France too,' said Alice, as they stared at a gold-covered Statue of Liberty.

'Perhaps in the cities,' said Louis. He dipped into his pocket and threw what looked suspiciously like a small button into the statue's top hat. The statue reached into the hat and flicked the button back towards Louis.

Alice couldn't help laughing at him. 'Serves you right,' she said. 'You're supposed to put actual money in.' She rummaged in her satchel for some coins and chucked them into the hat. The gold Statue of Liberty winked at her, then jerked back into position.

'I might have seen this sort of thing if I had ever lived near humans,' said Louis as they walked away. 'But where we live it is just mountains and monsters.'

'There's places like that in this country too,' said Alice, thinking about the trip Magnus had made recently to interview the stone giant. 'But less dangerous monsters are allowed to live in cities as well. There's tons of laws to stop them . . . I mean us . . . being seen.'

Louis pulled a face. 'I do not understand. What happens when you transform into a *loup-garou*?'

'Well, we don't, do we?' said Alice. 'Apart from the first time. We have to take the antidote. It's monster law.'

'Ah, *bien-sûr*. Of course,' said Louis, pressing the button at another crossing. 'I was forgetting you British werewolves must take this antidote.'

'Wait a minute!' Alice held on to Louis's arm to stop him tearing across the road before the lights changed. 'Do you mean you don't have to take it in France?'

He shook his head. 'Many choose not to. In my country, *les loup-garous* may run free with the full moon.'

Alice couldn't believe what she was hearing.

'I see you are shocked,' said Louis.

Too right I'm shocked! thought Alice. 'But what about killing other creatures or . . . you know . . . people?'

Louis laughed. 'My parents always eat a **gigantique** dinner before the moon comes out. That way, they do not feel the hunger. And anyway, most werewolves do not eat humans. They taste horrible.'

Alice stared at him. It was just as well the street was so noisy, because this conversation was getting weird. 'How do you know what humans taste like?'

'My *grandmère* told me that she tried one once and hated it. She said it tasted like cheap sausage.'

Alice made a mental note always to eat a huge meal on a full moon, just in case she lost her antidote. Thinking about her first transformation made her look at her hands. Her nails didn't seem to have grown at all since she last checked. Maybe her transformation wasn't imminent after all.

'When do you think your transformations might start?' she asked Louis.

He shook his head. '*Je ne sais pas*. My oldest brother transformed when he was fifteen, and my other brother at twelve.' He tugged a handful of his curls. 'But now my hair is growing so fast that I get it cut every week! So maybe it will start soon.' He shrugged. 'It is impossible to say.'

Alice bit her bottom lip. Should she ask? She decided yes. 'Do your brothers enjoy it? You know – being werewolves?'

Louis nodded vigorously. 'They love it!' he said.

'They roam the mountains with my parents and howl all night long. I just lie in my bed and listen to them. I cannot wait to join them.'

Alice couldn't believe being a werewolf in one country could be so different in another. She looked at Louis. This smiling, crazy-haired boy was actually going to be allowed to be a real werewolf.

And she never would.

6. MIRROR MIRROR

Alice tried to put thoughts about transforming or not transforming to the back of her mind. Lucille was expecting her to give Louis a tour of the city, so she decided to get on with it.

Thankfully, Louis seemed content with wandering the streets, staring at people and peering into shop windows. Alice wasn't really in the mood for sightseeing. Her encounter with Kiki was still bothering her. And although she was looking forward to the Nessies, and now even had a new friend to go with, she wasn't quite as excited as before.

After an hour of 'human watching', Alice realised

they'd skipped lunch. She led Louis into a supermarket.

'*Ooh la la!*' he exclaimed, running through the fruit and veg section. 'This is ***fantastique!*' In seconds his hands were full of bananas, carrots, tomatoes and strawberries, and he was chomping into them.

'Er, Louis?' said Alice, nervously looking around. 'The idea is to pay for the food first, then eat it.'

Louis stared at her, eyes bulging, mouth stuffed.

'It's OK,' she said, laughing. 'We'll get a basket and pay on the way out.'

Louis then set off, hurtling up and down the different aisles with Alice hot on his heels. It was like taking an alien on their first shopping trip. At the end of one aisle, they almost collided with a small group of shoppers crowded around a cooking demonstration. Standing on tiptoes, Alice could see a woman in a snazzy red apron grilling pieces of steak.

'Eat lean and clean with this meat grilling machine!'

she trilled into her clip-on microphone, handing round a tray of burnt steak morsels. Alice said a polite 'No thank you,' while Louis pulled a face.

'Blergh! Cooking meat is like killing it twice,' he told the woman.

Alice pushed him away. 'He's French,' she explained.

The woman pursed her lips. 'Thought so,' she snapped.

Alice quickly escorted Louis down another aisle. 'That was a bit rude,' she said.

He stared at her with wide, shocked eyes. 'But what this person did with the meat,' he said. 'It was terrible. It was burnt. Did you not smell it?' He stuck his tongue out and pinched his nose.

Alice gasped and went rigid, as still as the street performer before receiving the coins.

'No,' she said eventually. 'I didn't smell it. I can't smell anything.'

Alice spent the next few minutes charging around the supermarket frantically sniffing everything. She picked up bags of fresh coffee and inhaled what should have been a glorious just-roasted-bean aroma – but she smelled nothing. It was the same with the soaps – zero hint of fragrant floral freshness. At the cheese counter she leaned right over and virtually stuck her nose into a really ripe-looking blue cheese. It ought to have been so honking it made her eyes water.

Zilch. Not even the faintest whiff.

Panting as he caught up with her, Louis grabbed hold of her arm. '*Arrêt!* Stop! What is going on?'

Alice glared at him. 'It's my nose!' she hissed under her breath, so the suspicious cheese counter assistant couldn't hear. 'I can't smell anything.'

'Perhaps you have the cold?' suggested Louis.

'No! You're not getting it.'

'So tell me,' said Louis.

Alice suddenly felt like everyone in the queue for cheese was staring at her. She led Louis to the relative quiet of the cereal aisle.

'My werewolf power is super smellability,' she whispered, eyes darting around for eavesdroppers. 'Yours is hearing, isn't it?'

Louis coiled a strand of his hair around a finger. 'When was the last time you smelled something?'

Alice thought back. 'I remember thinking that Kiki smelled of a thousand different things.'

'And after that?'

'Exactly!' cried Alice. She jabbed Louis in the chest with a finger, possibly harder than she meant to. 'Nothing since then. Since Kiki touched me!'

'*Non*,' said Louis. 'Impossible!'

'Well something's happened to my super smellability,' said Alice, falling silent as a man walked past pushing a trolley. He looked at them oddly. It was impossible to talk about this in the supermarket. 'We should leave,' she said.

Alice smiled at the man, then led Louis towards the exit. She just wanted to get out. Her head was spinning and it couldn't cope with the supermarket's bright lights any longer.

Halfway down the tea and coffee aisle, there was someone hunched over a trolley piled high with shopping. As they got closer, the figure straightened up. The person had hair just like hers: bright ginger and cut into a bob. They were about her height, too.

'That's weird,' said Louis. 'That girl is wearing the same top as you. And the same sneakers.'

'I know,' said Alice, feeling a sudden shiver ripple through her.

Despite the urge to get out as fast as possible, Alice deliberately slowed as they approached the girl. She still had her back to them, and appeared to be ripping open packages of food. Plastic containers and cardboard sleeves littered the floor around her. There was a revolting gobbling and grunting noise, like a pig snuffling grubs out of the dirt. As Alice and Louis drew level, the girl began to turn.

Alice gasped and stared. Not just because there was a chunk of raw meat clasped between the girl's teeth. And not only due to the blood dripping from the corners of her mouth.

It was because that mouth and those teeth were on a familiar face. A *very* familiar face. The one she saw in the mirror every morning when she brushed her hair.

7. BOGOF

Alice gulped. Next to her, Louis gulped too. The lookie-likie Alice tossed her head back and swallowed the piece of meat like a heron devouring a flapping fish. Then *she* gulped as well. If Alice hadn't been so shocked at this exact replica of herself, even down to an identical rip on the knee of her skinny jeans, she'd have gagged at the horrible sight and sound of this other Alice guzzling down the meat.

The girl grabbed another pack of meat from the trolley. She ripped the plastic open with her teeth and pincered a raw chicken breast with her fingers.

'I know you're supposed to cook them first, but

I'm starving,' said the other Alice, chomping into the pink meat. She swallowed it down in one and belched. 'Naughty Alice,' she said, staring straight at the real Alice. '*You* shouldn't be eating meat *you* haven't paid for.' She wagged her finger. 'Tut tut! *You're* going to be in BIG trouble – especially when *you* do *this*!'

A momentary look of agony passed over the other Alice's face as her eyes became bloodshot and bulged like giant gobstoppers. Then her body tensed, as if struck by a bolt of lightning.

'*Mon dieu, non,*' whispered Louis. 'I have seen this before.'

Alice watched with growing horror. She'd seen something like this before too – when Magnus had transformed into a werewolf. Sure enough, the other Alice suddenly dropped to the floor, bright ginger hair sprouting from her hands, neck and cheeks. Her sneakers ripped apart around her hairy clawed feet, and her nose extended into a snarling muzzle. Sharp, glistening teeth dripping saliva on to the shiny supermarket floor.

The werewolf snarled, glaring at Alice with its grey-blue eyes. Then it winked, before leaping into the trolley and grabbing a huge slab of beef in its jaw. It ripped into the steak, spraying blood everywhere.

'Hey!' yelled a voice from towards the top end of the aisle. 'Stop your dog now or we're calling the police!'

Before Alice could react, the werewolf jumped off the trolley and bounded down the aisle, knocking over a display of fajita dinner kits and scattering boxes in all directions.

Without thinking, Alice charged after it. Behind her she could hear screaming, and Louis yelling at her to stop. But she didn't. She couldn't let this werewolf Alice get away. Nothing was going to stop her.

And nothing would have, if she hadn't careened

straight into the meat-grilling demonstration. Cooking utensils and shocked customers were sent flying. Amidst the chaos, Alice picked herself up and charged on, ignoring the screams and shouts. She hurtled after the werewolf, but the creature was too fast. Its powerful legs hurdled the self-service check-out machines, setting them all off in a simultaneous chorus of **'UNEXPECTED ITEM IN BAGGING AREA...'** It didn't even slow down as it bolted towards the exit. Alice could only watch in awe as it smashed through a window, soaring into the street in an explosion of glittering glass shards.

Alice burst out of the supermarket and searched the pavement for a glimpse of ginger fur, but the werewolf had vanished into the crowd of terrified-looking shoppers. Wow, werewolves were fast. And strong. And ate a LOT of meat! **Ew!**

'What *was* that?' asked a woman, her voice

quivering with fear.

'Some sort of wild dog, I think,' answered a man. 'Disgusting, letting a creature like that inside a supermarket.'

'And to think I bought my parsnips there last week!' said the woman. 'It probably escaped from the zoo or something. I expect they'll catch it eventually.'

'Or perhaps they'll just shoot the beast,' said the man. 'Can't have wild hounds terrorising the population.'

'Would they really just kill it?' asked Alice.

'You bet they would,' said the man, with an excited gleam in his eye. 'That dog was like some sort of monster! It should be shot, stuffed and stuck in a museum.'

Everyone nearby nodded and murmured in agreement.

Alice walked away into the crowd, head down, trying to focus on the pavement. Even though she couldn't make sense of what she'd just seen, shooting that creature didn't seem right.

A gap opened up ahead of her. But instead of a flash of ginger hair, she caught sight of a police officer's cap, its badge shining in the sunlight. Alice lowered her head to hide her face and ducked into the crowd.

Weaving her way through the heaving throng, Alice didn't have a clue where to go. She headed towards a side street, then felt a pull on her satchel. *They've caught me already!* she thought.

'Wait! *C'est moi!*' panted Louis, clutching his chest. 'It's me!'

'I'm not waiting to be arrested,' said Alice, weaving in and out of the other pedestrians.

'But you have done nothing wrong,' said Louis.

Alice stopped and caught her breath. 'You saw what I just saw, right?'

Louis nodded.

'Someone who looks exactly like me, eating a trolley-full of unpaid-for meat then turning into a werewolf?'

Louis bit his bottom lip and nodded.

'Good. Well, not good. Bad. Very bad.' Alice started walking at speed again. *At least I know I'm not seeing things*, she thought. Which wasn't much of a consolation.

'Where are we going?' asked Louis, sweat dripping down his forehead.

'Back to Jobs4Monsters,' said Alice. 'The supermarket will have called the police by now. What will I say if they catch me? That it was my totally identical twin that I never knew I had?' Alice's brain felt ready to explode. 'What's happening, Louis?'

Louis just shook his head and shrugged.

Just as they reached a junction, Alice spotted a pair of police officers racing towards them, batons in hand. She shoved Louis behind a group of tourists who were looking up at an old church tower.

'Ginger hair, blue top, they said on the radio!' shouted one police officer.

'Multiple offences, may be armed with a rabid dog!' yelled the other. **'Possible accomplice!'**

When the police had disappeared around the corner, Alice let out her breath.

'They are certainly making a big effort to find you,' said Louis as they hurried on down the road.

'And you,' said Alice. 'You're the accomplice they're talking about.'

They'd nearly made it back to Jobs4Monsters when a police van whizzed by, siren blaring and lights flashing. Alice dragged Louis into a newsagent's. It probably appeared dodgy to just wait by the door, so Alice went over to the counter and picked up some mints.

'Just these please,' she said. The man behind the till barely acknowledged her. He was too busy watching a news feed on his phone. Alice couldn't see the screen, but she could hear the reporter speaking. '. . . *police sources say the suspect had already targeted several other businesses in the city, destroying the entire stock of haggises from McInnerds Butchers and stealing a hundred kilos of Aberdeen Angus steaks. The girl and her male accomplice are thought to be radical vegetarians, having also disrupted a supermarket meat-grilling demonstration. The delinquent duo are believed to be feeding the pilfered prime cuts to their giant and dangerous dog . . .*'

The shopkeeper tutted. 'Disgusting behaviour,' he said, shaking his head. 'I've never trusted vegetarians.'

Alice picked up a pack of roast beef flavour crisps. 'I'll take these too,' she said, fumbling some coins on to the counter. 'Keep the change.'

Back outside, Alice handed Louis the crisps. 'You can have these,' she said, heading towards the alley behind Jobs4Monsters.

She led Louis into the office's back yard. But before she'd even bashed the bin, the lid flew open and Ronald's huge hairy head popped up.

'No entry!' the sasquatch growled. 'You can't go in.'

'What?' Alice spluttered. 'Why not?'

Ronald stared at Alice. 'Well, you *could* go in, but you'll be arrested by the MIA vampires if you do.'

'The who?'

'The MIA,' repeated Ronald. 'Monster Intelligence Agency. They monitor police activity in case naughty little monsters break human laws. They're inside looking for you.' He turned to Louis and smiled his stumpy yellow-toothed smile. '*Both* of you.'

8. WHERE HAVE YOU WHEELIE BIN?

Alice stared at the sasquatch. 'What should we do?'

Ronald crossed his long, hairy arms. 'Well,' he said slowly, 'you can either sit here like boobries and wait for them to drag you off to MonsterMax . . .'

'Or . . .?' said Alice, eyeing the door nervously. 'What's the or? There has to be an or.'

'. . . or,' continued Ronald, 'I suppose you could hide in my bin. Although I'm not sure harbouring wanted criminals is going to do much for my reputation for high-quality security services.'

'We're not criminals!' protested Alice.

'Maybe not,' said Ronald, 'but you *are* wanted.'

Alice shuddered at the thought of MonsterMax. She'd been locked up in a dungeon once before, and didn't much like the idea of going to prison. 'I think we'd better hide in your bin,' she said. 'Please, and thank you.' She stared at him for a moment. 'How do we get in?'

Ronald plucked Alice off the ground and dropped her into his bin. Seconds later, Louis was plonked next to her.

'It's . . . er . . . very cosy,' said Alice as Ronald squished her against Louis, who squeaked like a dog toy as he was forced further into a corner. 'Sorry,' she said, trying to give Louis a bit more room.

'*Merci*,' wheezed Louis.

Ronald pulled down the lid, plunging them into darkness. 'Quiet!' the sasquatch whispered. 'They're coming out.'

From inside the bin, Alice heard the door opening,

followed by a rasping, sinister voice.

'If we find that you have helped these underage usurpers of the law, the MIA will act swiftly and harshly. You will, quite literally, get it in the neck.'

Alice heard her uncle clearing his throat. 'And as *I* already said, I don't believe my niece was involved at all.'

There was a grating laugh which made Alice's skin prickle. She positioned her eye behind the sasquatch's peep hole, immediately stifling a cry.

Two tall, grey-faced figures towered over Magnus and Miss Pinky, casting long shadows over the yard. Their eyes were framed by dark rings and sharp teeth glinted in the corners of their mouths. Alice had never seen a vampire for real. They were even scarier than she'd imagined.

'We have a way of extracting the truth from even the most insolent children,' said one.

'And if she has violated the Ministry law on werewolf transformation,' said the other, 'we'll transport her to MonsterMax to face the most severe punishment.'

Both vampires flicked the collars on their deep purple cloaks up round their necks and turned to leave. One of them paused as he passed the bin. Alice held her breath as he sniffed the air. 'Might I suggest you get your bin emptied,' he said, his nostrils flaring. 'That smells worse than the congealed blood of a decapitated swamp troll.'

'Charming!' whispered the sasquatch. Thankfully the vampires didn't hear him.

'Phew!' said Miss Pinky, her whiskers twitching. 'Just looking at them makes my neck go all scratchy.'

'They weren't kidding, Miss Pinky,' said Magnus. 'If they run into Alice, her blood will be drained faster than you can say Transylvania.'

'Well then,' said Alice, 'we'd better make sure that

they *don't* run into me.'

'Who said that?' asked Miss Pinky.

'I did,' shouted Alice, her voice echoing around the bin.

'Those vampires really did make me go funny in the head,' said Miss Pinky. 'Because I could swear that bin just said something.'

Alice stood up inside the bin and pushed open the heavy lid. **'Surprise!'** she shouted.

She immediately wished she hadn't. Magnus just stood staring at her, shaking his head.

'It wasn't me. They've got it wrong!' cried Alice. Ronald gave her a leg-up and she scrambled over the side of the bin and ran over to Magnus. 'You have to believe me.'

'It *looks* like you in the police security footage,' said Miss Pinky, handing Alice her phone. 'See? That's you running out of a butcher's shop with what looks like

92

half a cow over your back. And here's you wearing a string of sausages around your neck. Not a good look.'

'It wasn't me,' shouted Alice. 'I swear!'

'What about this then?' asked Magnus, holding up his own phone. It was a CCTV image taken inside the supermarket just after Alice had destroyed the grilling demonstration. 'Are you saying that you *haven't* become a radical vegetarian?'

Alice bit her lip. If she'd been in court right now, standing in the dock, this would be a terrible start to her defence. 'Oh dear,' she said, wringing her hands. 'OK. That was me in the supermarket. But just because I'm vegetarian, doesn't mean I'm radical.'

Miss Pinky giggled. 'I've always thought you were a bit "rad".'

Alice looked at her. 'Not helpful, but thank you.'

'And there's this.' Magnus scrolled to a grainy image of a giant ginger wolf prowling through a bus station.

'That *definitely* can't be me,' Alice said. 'I'm still a Pre-T. How could I possibly transform into a werewolf? It's not even a full moon yet.'

'Of course I don't believe it was you,' Magnus said, placing a hand on her shoulder. 'And I've never heard of a werewolf transforming without a full moon. But you have to admit, this is all a bit crazy.'

'It's a lot crazy,' said Miss Pinky, earning her another glare.

'I know,' Alice said quietly. 'Weird things have been happening to me all day. First I lost my smellability—'

'What do you mean, lost it?' interrupted Magnus.

'Just that,' said Alice. 'It's gone. I can't smell a thing.'

'Since when?' asked Miss Pinky.

'I noticed it in the supermarket,' explained Alice. 'But I think it's been gone since I met Kiki.'

'Kiki!' exclaimed Magnus and Miss Pinky in unison.

'Yes.' Alice thought back to the very odd sensation

when Kiki had grabbed her hands. 'Something strange happened at that press conference.'

'*Oui*,' said Louis, jumping out of the bin and joining Alice. 'It did. I saw it too.'

'You must be Louis,' said Magnus. He shook Louis's hand. 'Miss Pinky told me about Alice meeting you at the press conference. Which, incidentally,' he said, turning back to Alice, 'you were not supposed to be at!'

Alice winced. 'Sorry.'

'If you hadn't both sneaked out in the first place,' said Magnus, 'we wouldn't be in this mess now.' He sighed. 'So who's this person in all these police photos?'

'That's the next crazy thing,' said Alice. 'My exact double appearing like that. We watched her transform into a werewolf right in the middle of a crowded supermarket!'

'She was pushing a trolley full of meat,' confirmed Louis.

'I would never do that. I'm a vegetarian!' said Alice.

'A radical vegetarian,' said Miss Pinky.

Alice threw one of her extra-strength glare bombs at Miss Pinky.

Magnus paced around the yard for a moment. 'We need to do two things,' he said. 'Find out why you've lost your smellability, and who this double is. Agreed?'

Everyone agreed. Even Ronald grunted a 'yes' from inside his bin.

'More important than all that though,' Magnus added, 'is to hide you both.'

'*Moi aussi?*' asked Louis. 'What about my *maman*? She will be worried.'

Magnus shook his head. 'We can't risk the MIA finding either of you. Not until we know what's going on. Them thinking Alice transformed into a werewolf is bad enough, but doing it in public … If they catch her, they'll never set her free.'

'But it wasn't me!' cried Alice. 'And I'm sure nobody apart from me and Louis saw her transform.'

'Do you fancy convincing those vampires?' asked Magnus.

Alice shook her head. No way did she want to try that.

'Look,' said Magnus. 'Those vampires are after your blood. Literally. We have to get you out of sight and smell, and fast. I'll get hold of your mother, Louis. Make sure she understands the situation.'

'*Merci, Monsieur Magnus.*'

Alice's mind was spinning. How could everything have changed so quickly? Then her stomach and heart and pretty much everything inside her felt like it dropped to the ground. 'The Nessies!' she cried. 'I can't go if I'm in hiding, can I?'

Silence fell over the yard. It even sounded like the wind had stopped blowing. Magnus's face told Alice the answer.

'Too risky,' he said. 'Those vampires will certainly look for you there.' He gave Alice a big hug. 'I know how much you were looking forward to it.'

Alice sniffed. Everything went blurry and she wiped her eyes with her sleeve.

'If Alice isn't going, neither am I,' Miss Pinky said.

Alice felt awful. The Nessies was the most glamorous night in the monster calendar. In other words, Miss Pinky heaven. 'You don't need to miss it just because of me,' she said.

Miss Pinky rushed over and gave her a hug. 'Some things are more important than hanging out with monster celebrities,' she said.

'Am I one of them?' Alice asked.

'No,' said Miss Pinky, making Alice gasp. 'You're the

only thing more important than that!'

Alice hugged her back. 'Thank you,' she said. 'But where are we going to hide from the MIA?'

'You can't stay in the office,' said Miss Pinky. 'Those vampires are bound to be back and they looked thirsty.'

'They might search our flats too,' said Magnus.

'What about Doogie's place?' asked Alice.

Magnus shook his head. 'It won't take the MIA to work out he's my boyfriend, so they'll probably search his flat as well. It needs to be somewhere the human police won't think of looking either.'

Alice slumped back against the bin. 'I forgot I was on their wanted list as well.'

'Oi!' echoed Ronald's deep voice from inside. 'I'm trying to have a kip in here.'

'Brainwave!' said Miss Pinky. 'You could hide in the bin again.'

The lid flew open and Ronald jumped up like a hairy

jack-in-the-box. 'No way!' he boomed.

Alice agreed. 'No offence Ronald, but it's too pokey in there. A girl's gotta breathe.'

'This *garçon* too,' said Louis.

Just then, Dustin's dust-covered head poked out from the office back door. Everyone turned towards him.

'Can I go home now please?' said the brownie. He picked a long cobweb off his body and shoved it into his mouth, sucking it up like spaghetti. 'What? I'm hungry. With those vampires in the office I missed my tea break.'

Magnus rolled his eyes. 'Yes Dustin, you can go home.'

The brownie grunted and whirled out into the yard.

'Hey!' cried Magnus. 'Hold on a minute! Aren't brownies' homes enchanted?'

Dustin pulled apart his fringe, his tiny black eyes

peering out into the sunlight. 'Yes,' he said, with a wary edge to his voice. 'We can make ourselves and our homes invisible. Why?'

Magnus and Miss Pinky exchanged looks.

'Great!' cheered Miss Pinky. 'That's sorted then!' She smiled at Alice and Louis. 'You might not find it on Scare B&B, but it looks like you two are bunking with a brownie tonight.'

9. DUST BUSTING

The first thing Alice noticed about Dustin's flat, which was only a few minutes' walk from Jobs4Monsters, was that she hardly noticed it at all. She and Louis had walked right past his front door without even seeing it. Ivy grew over the building, almost covering the windows and door. Dustin opened the door and disappeared from sight.

'Do you think it really is enchanted?' Alice asked Louis.

Louis nodded. '*Oui*. And I think he is too. Not one person noticed him the whole way here.'

It was true. Dustin may have been only four feet tall,

but he was covered from head to toe in hair. *Everyone* should have noticed him. But it appeared that the brownie and his home both had the ability to hide in plain sight.

'Take your shoes off,' shouted Dustin as they closed the door behind them.

Alice and Louis removed their shoes and padded after Dustin in their socks, through to his living room. Alice gasped. She'd expected something dark and dingy and dust-covered. But it was airy and bright and one hundred percent dust free. Every picture frame gleamed, every lightshade sparkled. The carpet had been vacuumed like a perfectly manicured lawn. It even had stripes.

'It smells so clean!' whispered Louis.

'I wouldn't know,' said Alice. Then she spotted the books. 'Wow! Are these all yours, Dustin?'

The brownie pushed his fringe aside and fixed her with a beady-eyed stare. 'Don't sound so surprised,' he said. 'Just because I clean for a living doesn't mean I can't read.' He let go of his hair, which closed over his eyes like an old-fashioned theatre curtain.

'Sorry, Dustin.' Alice tilted her head sideways to examine the books' spines. 'This looks interesting,' she said, pulling out an ancient leather-bound volume titled *Ninth Century Dragon Classification in the Highlands*. The book next to that was *Island Mermaid Clans – Territorial Disputes of the Ancient Era*. She showed it to Louis. 'I thought mermaids were supposed to be nice.'

The ones she'd met before had seemed friendly.

Dustin laughed gruffly from behind his fringe. 'You've obviously never studied the Great Mermaid War of 1841.'

'Er . . . no. That's definitely not on our curriculum,' said Alice. 'Do monsters learn about that sort of stuff at school?'

Dustin shook his head, which sent dust tumbling on to the pristine carpet. 'Actually, I don't think I studied that until university.'

Alice was careful not to sound too surprised this time. 'What did you study at university?'

'Ancient Monster History,' said Dustin, proudly. A pink arm popped out from under his hair and pointed to a gold embossed certificate hanging on the wall. 'Double first class with extra honours.'

'And you are working as a cleaner?' Louis laughed. 'That's crazy!'

'There aren't many jobs around for monster historians,' said Dustin, shaking his head and sending even more dust raining down. 'I just took the first thing that came up.'

Alice looked around the room. 'I thought you were a terrible cleaner, but this place is way less dusty than Jobs4Monsters.'

Dustin laughed. 'I *am* a terrible cleaner. I have another house brownie come in once a week to tidy my flat.'

'You're a cleaner with a cleaner?' asked Louis. 'That really *is* crazy!'

Dustin led them into his kitchen, which was also spotlessly clean, and bustled about getting supper ready. He ladled out three bowls of soup, then sat down and began slurping noisily.

Alice glanced into her bowl. The soup was brown and water-thin and there were balls of soggy stuff and other UFOs floating in it. It was one of Alice's rules in life never to eat an Unidentified Food Object, and she wasn't going to break it now.

Dustin noticed her hesitation. He jumped down from his chair and fetched a tin from the counter. 'Try these instead,' he said.

Alice peered into the tin. Inside were blueish-grey biscuits, the colour of tumble-dryer fluff. She held one up between her fingers. Like the soup, she was pretty sure that it was made of dust.

Dustin continued slurping away happily, while Alice and Louis pretended to nibble their dust biscuits. Alice tried hard not to think about the Nessies and her smellability and the other Alice, but everything jumbled together in her brain, clamouring to be heard. By the time Dustin was on his third bowl, she'd had enough.

'I can't just sit here and pretend that nothing

has happened,' she said suddenly. Dustin's spoon clattered in his bowl and Louis dropped the biscuit he was holding. 'I need to DO something.'

'Right then,' said Dustin, shoving his bowl to one side. 'Let's approach this academically. What are the facts? You have lost your sense of smell and discovered you have a double who turned herself into a werewolf. Is this correct?'

Alice nodded. She was impressed. This was not the Dustin who'd been creating dust chaos in the office all week.

'How about we look at the "double you" situation first?' suggested Dustin. 'It's all a question of angles. How we approach the problem is just as important as solving it.'

Alice and Louis shared 'What's he on about?' glances.

'For example,' continued Dustin. 'What if this other

Alice hasn't always been another Alice?'

Alice and Louis must have stared at Dustin like he was speaking in ancient mermish, because he made a frustrated squeaking noise. 'What I mean is this,' he said. 'What if she's only just become your double?'

'*Zut alors!*' exclaimed Louis. 'You mean this person changed to look like Alice?'

'Precisely,' said Dustin.

Alice had heard about people changing their identities and starting new lives, but why would they want to look like her? 'That would take a lot of plastic surgery,' she said.

Dustin tutted and waggled a finger at her. 'You're thinking like a human. You need to think more like a monster.'

Alice thought hard. 'What if my double *is* a monster?'

Dustin chuckled. 'Very good. Go on.'

'A monster who transformed to look like me?'

'Indeed.' Dustin had pulled his fringe open again and was staring at her intently. 'Perhaps even to *be* you.'

Alice shuddered. The idea that there was this other Alice out there was just too creepy. 'Is there such a thing?' she asked.

Dustin jumped down from the table. 'Of course,' he said. 'Shapeshifters. Like both of you.'

'What?'

'*Quoi?*'

'Werewolves are shapeshifters,' said Dustin. 'One day, you will both be able to turn into something else.'

'That's if I'm still allowed to be a werewolf,' said Alice.

'I have never heard of a creature who steals another person's identity,' said Louis.

'That's because *you* don't have a double first in ancient monster history,' said Dustin. He bustled out of the kitchen and into the living room, where he began heaving books down from the shelves. Before long he hurried back in, struggling under the weight of a tatty old encyclopaedia.

'If I remember correctly,' he said, leafing through the pages, 'ancient monster lore talked of shapeshifters that could mimic other creatures. They were quite common centuries ago.'

'Could one of them be powerful enough to transform into a werewolf without a full moon?' asked Alice.

Dustin shrugged. 'I don't remember reading anything like that.'

'But they still exist, these shapeshifters?'

'In theory, yes,' said Dustin.

'But it's unlikely,' said Alice. 'Is that what you were going to say?'

Dustin heaved the book to the middle of the table and went back into the living room, returning with a

teetering pile of books and papers. 'Unlikely isn't the same as definitely not,' he said. He glanced at the clock on the kitchen wall. 'Bedtime,' he said. 'You can take my room. I'm going to stay up and do some research.'

Dustin's bedroom was as clean as the rest of his flat, It looked like his bed had never been slept in. Alice lay in it, staring at the ceiling.

'You are not sleeping?' whispered Louis from his makeshift bed on the floor.

'Can't,' replied Alice.

'*Alors*,' he said, jumping up and sitting on the end of the bed, cross-legged. His eyes sparkled orange in the near-darkness. 'Talk to me.'

Alice sat up and looked at him. 'I just don't see the point,' she said. 'No amount of research is going to get my smellability back. I'm probably not even a werewolf any more. If Dustin's right about this shapeshifter, maybe she's taken my werewolf ability as well. We watched her transform, didn't we? I might as well go home, forget about all this and be normal again.'

Louis tooth-whistled. 'Normal as in human? That sounds boring.'

'It might be boring, but at least it's not so complicated,' Alice groaned. 'I don't know who I am any more.'

'You are a werewolf, Alice,' said Louis firmly. 'Do you not want the chance to know what it feels like to transform? To become the thing you were born to be? I know I do.'

'This isn't France, Louis,' Alice said. 'I won't be allowed to transform. Even if I still can.' She rolled over to face the wall. Sleeping seemed impossible, so she concentrated on Louis's breaths coming from the floor. When he started snoring gently, she began counting them instead, and eventually she felt herself drifting off.

10. AN ANCIENT WARNING

When Alice woke up, it took a while for her to work out why it was so quiet. Then she realised. Louis wasn't snoring. Sitting up in bed, she looked down at the floor. He wasn't there.

She got up and headed towards the living room, where she could hear her friend talking to Dustin. *That's good*, she thought. *I can tell them both at the same time.*

'*Bonjour!*' chirruped Louis, sounding surprisingly cheerful.

'Morning!' said Dustin, yawning. All of his body hair was knotted and matted. He'd pegged his fringe up on either side and was rubbing his eyes. He was surrounded by books.

'Guys,' Alice announced. 'I've made a decision. I'm going to go back home.'

'We have found something,' said Louis, completely ignoring her.

Dustin coughed in a very pointed way.

'Sorry.' Louis bowed to the brownie. 'I mean, Dustin has found something.'

Dustin handed Alice a flimsy booklet. 'I found it a couple of hours ago,' he said. 'It was hidden inside an old dictionary.'

The document looked ancient, printed on some sort of skin. The ink was the red-brown colour of dried blood, and it was faded. Alice opened the curtain and held it up to the daylight.

The Kronikel of the Karamorph

(PARTIALLY TRANSLATED FROM THE ANCIENT RUNES)

The Karamorph is born to steal ~
Your life-force her next gruesome meal.
Victims chosen for their power
Are left as but a drooping flower.

With hands of doom she grasps her prey
To drain their very life away.
To change her shape her greatest aim,
Your suffering is part of the game.

Alice carefully turned the page, but the rest of the booklet was blank.

'The translation was never finished,' said Dustin. 'We don't know the rest.'

Alice flipped back to the beginning and re-read the lines again.

Then again.

A thousand icy pinpricks punctured her skin.

'This happened to me,' she said, the booklet shaking in her hand. 'At the press conference. Kiki grasped my hands and tried to drain me! That's exactly what it felt like.'

Louis tapped Dustin on the head. '*Voilà!* Told you,' he said.

Alice's brain was crammed full again, but now it all made sense.

'Kiki did this to me,' she said. 'She drained me so she could *become* me. Which means my double is Kiki,

because Kiki is the shapeshifter. This Karamorph –
it's Kiki!'

All thoughts of going home were banished. Alice
slumped into an armchair. Her heart was racing, her
mind whirring and her hands were still shaking. She
looked up at Dustin. 'Why is she doing this?'

Dustin scratched his head. 'We don't know.'

'If only we had the rest of this *Kronikel*,' said Alice.
'That might tell us.'

'We do,' said Dustin, rifling through some more
papers scattered across the floor. 'I found this with the
translation. Careful, though – it's delicate.'

Alice took the thin parchment gingerly in her
fingers. It was creased and torn, and as fine as lace in
places. Strange symbols and marks covered one side.
Alice could just make out an illustration of a figure with
hands outstretched. Lines emanated from its fingers,
like light . . . or energy.

'Is this the *Kronikel*?' Alice asked. She stared at it as if the symbols might start moving on the page.

'I think so,' said Dustin. 'Written in ancient monster runes.'

'If only we knew what it said.' Alice puffed out her cheeks. 'We could work out why this Karamorph or Kiki or whoever is doing this.' She paused and breathed in deeply. 'And whether I can get my werewolf powers back.'

Dustin tapped a massive book on the floor with his big toe. 'I might be able to help,' he said. 'I took a course at university in ancient rune translation, and I've still got this old rune dictionary.'

Alice smiled. 'Brilliant! So you're an expert on this.'

Dustin coughed. 'Not exactly. That's the one course I failed.'

'Oh.' Alice frowned. 'How long will it take you to become an expert?'

'How long have I got?' asked Dustin.

Alice looked at her watch. 'Until about six o'clock this evening.'

Dustin sighed. 'I'll get cracking.' He grabbed the ancient dictionary, sat down with his legs crossed underneath a curtain of hair, and heaved the book up into his lap.

Alice and Louis went into the kitchen in search of breakfast, promising to bring Dustin some too. A quick rummage confirmed that breakfast was going to consist of dust toast and some grey jam Alice found in the fridge. To be fair, the brownie hadn't been expecting guests.

They took a plate of toast to Dustin, who was lying face-down in his books. Alice nudged him gently. He snorted and sat bolt upright.

'I wasn't sleeping. I was thinking,' he said, rummaging for his notebook.

'I've been thinking too,' said Alice as she and Louis sat down. 'Even if you can work out what those runes say, we'll still have to convince everyone else that Kiki is this Karamorph. Who's going to listen to a radical vegetarian wanted by the police and the MIA?'

'Good point,' said Louis.

'There must be some way of proving Kiki isn't who she says she is.' Alice thought for a moment. 'I read a book about witches once. Didn't they used to dunk someone they suspected of witchcraft in a pond? If they drowned, they weren't a witch. If they survived, they threw them on the fire?'

Dustin yawned. 'Sorry,' he said. 'Historically, monsters have used a different method to prove witchery. They concoct a batch of *serum reveletarium*, throw it over the suspected witch and see what happens.'

Alice liked the sound of this. 'What does happen?'

'Nothing. Zilch. *Nada*,' said Dustin. 'There's no records of it working.'

Alice picked up a slice of dust toast without thinking and bit into it. She peeled a piece of fluff off her tongue. 'What about records of it *not* working?'

Dustin shrugged. 'None of them either.'

'So there are no records at all?'

'Not that I know of,' said Dustin. 'What are you getting at?'

Alice stood up. 'If there's no records either way, there's a chance this serum revele-whatever actually could work.'

Louis whistled. '*Très bien*, Alice. Very clever.'

'Not clever,' said Alice. 'Logical.'

Dustin swallowed his toast and licked his lips. 'Your logic is a bit wacky,' he said. 'To prove your theory you'd need the serum, and for that you'd need a really good monster apothecary.'

'Is an apothecary like a chemist?' asked Alice.

'Yes,' said Dustin. 'Don't tell me you know one?'

Alice smiled. 'No. But I know someone who does . . .'

'Never fear, Pinky's here!' announced Miss Pinky a short while later, as Dustin let her in. 'I'd have got here sooner, only I couldn't find your door, Dustin. And there were a couple of police officers lurking around the corner.'

She threw a paper bag to Alice. 'Breakfast,' she said, smiling. 'As requested.'

'Who requested breakfast?' asked Dustin. 'We've already had some.'

Miss Pinky held out her phone. The screen said:

Get here pronto. Bring muffins.

Alice put her hand up. 'That was me,' she said. 'I borrowed your phone, Dustin. Sorry, but I just can't eat your dust food.'

She bit a huge chunk out of one of the muffins and chewed it hopefully for a moment, before remembering that taste went with smellability. She sighed, then explained everything that they'd discovered. Miss Pinky's eyes grew wider and wider by the second.

'That's a triple wowser with a side of epic!' said Miss Pinky.

'I know,' said Alice. 'So we need to find someone to make up this serum and I thought maybe your friend at MonLab might help us.'

Miss Pinky tapped her phone. 'If anyone can make this serum, Jeanie can.'

Alice checked her watch. 'But we're running out of time. And we have to get to the Nessies.'

Miss Pinky mewed. 'Are you still going?'

'Of course,' said Alice. 'If we can get hold of the serum fast enough. The Nessies will be the one place we know this Karamorph will be.'

'So the Kiki at the press conference wasn't Kiki after all,' said Miss Pinky. 'You said she didn't seem like herself, Alice.'

'Whatever she did to me,' said Alice, 'I bet she did it to Kiki too.'

'And who knows how many others over the centuries?' said Dustin.

'That thing took my smellability,' said Alice firmly. 'And I want it back. Everyone thinks I've illegally transformed into a werewolf because of her. There's no way I'm spending the rest of my life eating MonsterMax prison slop.'

Miss Pinky hugged Alice. 'I'm so pleased you haven't given up,' she said. 'I know you'd never dream of doing a thing like that, but still . . .'

Alice could feel herself blushing. To think she'd almost gone home!

'This could be dangerous,' said Miss Pinky, licking her whiskers. 'We'll need to be very brave.'

Alice looked at her. 'You mean like last time?'

Louis laughed. 'Does this sort of thing always happen to you two?'

Alice shrugged. 'So far, yes,' she said. 'And we should let Magnus and Doogie know, so they can meet us there. We'll need as many people on our side as possible.'

'*Et ma mère?*' asked Louis. 'What about her?'

'Magnus spoke to your mum and explained everything,' said Miss Pinky. 'I'll call Jobs4Monsters now and tell Magnus what's happening!' Her phone pinged as she picked it up. 'That's Jeanie. She's expecting us.'

Louis was literally licking his muffin case clean

while Dustin had just fallen asleep on top of his rune dictionary.

'Come on you two!' said Alice. 'We're going on a mission.'

Let's just hope we don't run into the police or the MIA vampires first.

11. SECURITY ➡
CLEARANCE LEVEL THREE

'Are you sure this is necessary?' Alice pinched her nose to try to stop yet another sneeze from escaping, but it was no use. 'Achoo!' A mini explosion of dust fired from her mouth. She looked down at her dust-covered clothes. 'This was my favourite top,' she said, glumly.

Miss Pinky's bright blue eyes were the only thing Alice recognised under the thick covering of grey powder Dustin had coated them all in. Even her whiskers had a light frosting of grey.

'When you said this stuff worked like magic, Dustin,' said Miss Pinky, 'did you mean like pulling rarebits out of bats?'

'Don't you mean rabbits out of hats?' asked Alice.

'No, I mean rarebits,' said Miss Pinky. 'They're a type of forest troll. Favourite snack of the sharp-nosed Dragbat.'

'*Oh la la!*' Louis shook his head, instantly shrouding himself in a grey cloud. His curls seemed to hold way more dust than anyone else's hair. He coughed as the cloud cleared. 'It does not taste very magical,' he spluttered.

'It's not exactly magic,' said Dustin. 'You'll just have to trust me.'

Louis looked at Alice. 'He does have a double first degree.'

'Maybe, but I'm sure a taxi would have been easier,' muttered Alice.

'And risk being recognised?' Miss Pinky pointed to a shop window. 'Look!'

A poster had been stuck to the inside of the glass.

HAVE YOU SEEN THIS GIRL? it said in big red letters. **WANTED FOR MEAT-RELATED CRIMES!** There was also a horrible photo of Alice gorging herself on a giant slab of raw liver.

Alice shuddered. 'I look terrible in that photo!' she cried. 'And it's not even me! Who's going to believe me now when I say I'm a vegetarian?'

MonLab was on the south side of the city. As they headed that way, Alice kept an eye out for vampires, but it was the human police they spotted first. A pair of young officers stood chatting on the street. Alice froze to the spot.

'Don't panic,' said Dustin. 'We'll use some brownie mind-control. It's another way we have stayed hidden from humans for so long.' He began chanting quietly under his breath. *'We're not here, we're not there, you can't see us anywhere.'* He paused for a moment. 'Join in, everyone!'

He repeated the chant a few times. Then Miss Pinky started as well, followed by Louis. Alice thought it was ridiculous, but the others seemed convinced, so she began too.

'We're not here, we're not there, you can't see us anywhere.' They all whispered the chant as they walked past the officers. It felt like the officers' eyes were

boring into Alice's back like lasers, but the police didn't stop them.

'Wow! It worked!' Alice was seriously impressed.

Dustin didn't say anything. Alice thought she could hear him chuckling.

'None of this actually works, does it?' she said, realising. 'The dust? The chanting?'

'The dust made you unrecognisable,' said Dustin. 'So that worked.'

'And the silly chanting?' asked Louis.

'I thought it would take your minds off the police.' Dustin lifted his hat and winked at Alice. 'Sometimes you only have to believe something will work, and it does.'

They soon found themselves walking through an industrial estate full of huge grey buildings.

Miss Pinky led them towards a building right at the far end. 'MonLab's in there,' she said. 'Well, technically, it's *under* there. You'll see.'

Alice peered up at the dull-looking block. It didn't look much like a laboratory. She craned her neck for a better look, promptly tripping over the edge of the pavement and sprawling on the ground.

'Ouch!' She climbed back to her feet and looked at her palms. 'I'm bleeding,' she said. 'Anyone got a hanky?'

'*Désastre*!' gasped Louis, staring goggle-eyed at Alice.

'If that means disaster,' said Miss Pinky with a mew, 'then yes. It is.'

'What's the big deal? It's just a scratch,' said Alice.

'One word,' said Dustin. 'Vampires!'

'What about them?'

'What about them!' Miss Pinky started hopping on her paws. 'When you registered with the Ministry you had to give them a blood sample, right?'

'Right,' said Alice, with a Titanic-sized sinking feeling in her tummy.

'So they have your blood on their database,' continued Dustin.

'There's a reason they employ vampires at the MIA,' said Miss Pinky.

'*Oui*,' said Louis. 'They can sniff out blood from miles away.'

Alice felt sick. She frantically wiped her hands on her jeans.

'Too late,' groaned Miss Pinky. 'They'll be on to you in no time. We have to hurry. Come on!'

She disappeared around the side of the building. Alice and the others followed. Dustin brought up the rear, huffing and puffing under the weight of the enormous rune dictionary.

'In here, quick!'

Miss Pinky was holding open a door. They all trooped in and began descending a really long spiral staircase. After a dizzying number of twists, they came to a dark-looking tunnel at the bottom. There was a faint light somewhere up ahead. Everyone held on to each other as they walked slowly towards it.

'*Beurk!*' exclaimed Louis somewhere behind Alice. 'This smell is terrible.'

'You're not wrong Louis,' said Miss Pinky. 'It smells worse than centaur farts.'

Alice wished they would stop going on about the smell. She'd do anything to be able to sniff it, no matter how pongy it was.

'A giant guffworm works here,' explained Miss Pinky. 'Jobs4Monsters found him the job last year.'

Alice burst out laughing. 'You're making that up!'

'I am not,' protested Miss Pinky. 'The guffworm is the lab's main power source. Just don't ask which end they extract the power from.'

The moment she said this, the tunnel was suddenly flooded with bright, white light. A piercing alarm sounded, followed by a robotic-sounding voice.
'SECURITY ALERT! INTRUDERS DETECTED!'

Up ahead, a metal door began to slide open. Behind it was a narrow room, with another door at the far end.

'Walk forward!' blared a voice. **'Hands where we can see them!'**

Heart pounding, Alice held her hands up over her head as they shuffled into the room. Behind them, the first door slid shut.

'They've updated their security protocol since my last visit,' said Miss Pinky, sounding nervous.

'*Silence!*' yelled the voice. A spy hole in the door

flickered. Someone – or something – was watching them. Above the spy hole was a sign.

I don't like the sound of that, thought Alice.

Another sudden clanking noise made her jump. She wouldn't have been surprised if the floor dropped away, sending them all tumbling into a pit of guffworms.

Instead, the door began to rise into the ceiling.

Bit by bit, the rising door revealed two humungous hairy feet, equally hairy legs, and a long torso covered in white matted fur. Alice held her breath as a bearded chin and large head came into view. Piercing turquoise eyes shone out from under a black peaked cap, pinned to which was a shiny silver badge. Alice could make out the letters *Y.E.S.* on it. The creature looked like a white-haired version of Ronald, or the Big Foot from the press conference.

'Names! Monster type! Purpose of visit!' it roared powerfully.

They all quickly stated their names and monster category.

'We need to speak to Jeanie,' said Miss Pinky. 'In the anti-venom laboratory.'

'Why?' yelled the creature.

'It's a secret emergency,' said Miss Pinky. She winked at Alice.

'That's not going to help,' Alice whispered. Ignoring her jelly-legs as best she could, she turned to the monster. 'Hi!' she began. 'Your colleague let us into the Nessies' press conference yesterday. We have top-level security clearance.'

Miss Pinky mewed quietly. 'Uh oh . . .'

'I don't have a colleague,' growled the monster.

'But the security guard yesterday looked like you,' said Alice. 'He was another Big Foot.'

Miss Pinky mewed again, only this time more loudly. 'You've done it now,' she said.

The monster took a massive step towards them, flexing its toes so that they all cracked. It brought its eyes so close to Alice's face that she could see the tiny veins in them. In a low, measured voice, each word separated by a deep intake of breath, it said, 'I. Am. Not. A. Big. Foot.'

'You're not?' Alice winced as the creature shook its head slowly. 'How about a sasquatch?'

The monster's eyes narrowed. 'Try again.'

Alice couldn't afford another wrong guess. 'I know!'

she cried, suddenly remembering. 'You're a yeti!'

The yeti stepped back. 'I suppose you think we all look the same, don't you?'

'Actually,' said Alice, 'you're way more scary.' She hoped she'd said the right thing.

The yeti stroked his long chin. Then he stepped aside. 'Anti-venom department's four floors down.' He reached behind him and handed them each a piece of paper. 'Feedback forms,' he said. 'We at Yeti Excellent Security value your opinion.'

Everyone shuffled past the yeti. Alice turned back. 'That's a very smart cap you're wearing,' she said.

The yeti beamed a yellow-toothed smile. 'Thank you,' it roared. 'And remember, if you need any security services, my motto is, **"If you're in a mess, just say Y.E.S.!"'**

12. BUBBLE BUBBLE ~ WE'VE GOT TROUBLE

Miss Pinky led them into a cage-like lift and pressed a button marked **-4**. They rattled down for what felt like miles, until the door opened on to a massive laboratory. Long white workbenches covered in gleaming jars were connected to giant vats by bubbling glass tubes. Flames flickered everywhere, boiling up green-coloured liquids here and red-coloured ones there. Monsters in white coats wandered around tapping into devices or stopping to observe experiments. Most wore face masks so it was impossible to distinguish exactly what type of monsters they were, although Alice spotted two with faun-like horns, and one with a trailing snake's tail. Behind one bench there was even a centaur, who wore a white sheet over his horse's body. Every glass and metal surface gleamed.

'Wow!' exclaimed Dustin. 'It's cleaner than my flat.'

Alice brushed some dust off her clothes. 'It won't be for long now we're here.'

Miss Pinky reached for some lab coats hanging on hooks by the lift. 'We'd better cover up then,' she said, handing everyone a coat. 'You too, Dustin,' she said, selecting a small one for the brownie.

'How are you getting on with the runes?' asked Alice, holding the dictionary for Dustin.

'When exactly have I had time to study them?' he asked as he put on the coat. 'So far all I've done is carry this breeze-block of a book around like I'm in training for the monster marines.'

'Let's find Jeanie,' said Miss Pinky, leading them through the lab.

Alice half-expected to be stopped by more security guards at any moment, or at least challenged by one of the lab technicians, but nobody even gave them a second glance. The monster chemists were far too engrossed in their experiments or busy at their computer terminals to notice four rather dusty strangers wandering through their workspace.

At the end of the vast laboratory, a sort of mist was swirling around. Smoky tendrils rolled over the workbench and on to the floor where they formed a reddish miasma.

'That'll be her,' said Miss Pinky.

Sure enough, the red mist instantly gathered into a column of smoke which transformed into a white-coated woman, whose face was almost entirely covered by giant-sized goggles. She was also wearing a purple headscarf, which seemed to be smouldering slightly. She took off her goggles, revealing dark brown eyes,

and immediately set about tamping out her smoking scarf.

'That's the third scarf this week I've singed on a Bunsen burner,' she said. 'I really should be more careful.' She smiled. 'Hi everyone! I'm Jeanie.'

Alice introduced herself, followed by the others. Jeanie shrank to Dustin's level to shake his hand without even bending her knees, and then expanded again before leading them to her workstation. She wobbled slightly as she walked.

'As you can see,' said Jeanie, 'I'm very much a genie with a limp.'

'Don't you mean a lamp?' asked Alice.

'No, I mean a limp. I dropped a demijohn of wolfsbane extract on my big toe yesterday and you wouldn't believe the pain!'

'Oh,' said Alice. 'But do you live in a lamp?'

Miss Pinky sniggered. 'That's hilarious!'

Alice thought it was a totally reasonable question to ask a genie.

'No, I don't live in a lamp,' said Jeanie. 'Nor can I grant you three wishes. These are both stories made up for human entertainment.'

A blush flooded Alice's face. If she was going to keep making silly mistakes like that, maybe it *was* best if she wasn't a monster any more.

Jeanie smiled. 'I do, however, live in a bottle.' She pointed to a tall clear glass bottle on a shelf behind the bench. 'It's an old elderflower cordial bottle. Reduce, reuse, recycle, and all that. I shrink myself to fit into it, and when I fancy a change, I take it to the bottle bank and choose a different one.'

'It looks very homely,' said Alice, trying not to embarrass herself again.

As Louis peered at the vials and jars of weird-coloured things lined up on Jeanie's workbench, Dustin settled underneath it and opened the dictionary.

'He's translating ancient monster runes,' explained Alice.

'Sounds intriguing,' said Jeanie. 'Tell me everything you know.'

Alice knew time was against them. She gave Jeanie a quick recap of everything that had happened at the press conference and since. For a brief moment she worried it sounded too far-fetched, but Jeanie didn't even raise an eyebrow.

'First we need a recipe for the serum,' said the genie. She dissolved back into mist, this time a sort of orangey colour. 'Found it!' she said, reappearing with a large, dog-eared book. 'It was in the Unproven Formula section.'

'Oh dear,' said Alice. 'That's not very hopeful.'

'I've certainly never tried to make it before,' said Jeanie. 'But I love a challenge!' With that, she changed into a swirling coil of yellow mist and disappeared through the floor.

Alice looked at Miss Pinky. 'It's not going to work, is it?'

'Rubbish!' Miss Pinky picked up some goggles and peered through them, making her eyes look twice their normal size. 'Jeanie's a total boffin. If anyone can do it, she can.'

'Did someone say boffin?'

Jeanie had reappeared again with a basket of jars,

packets and boxes with labels peeling off them. 'I had to go into the vault for some of this,' she said, laying it out on the bench. She sneezed. 'It could do with a dust down there.'

'Don't look at me,' came Dustin's voice from under the bench.

Jeanie measured out powders, grated bits of what looked like tree bark and counted out drops of sludge-like liquids. It all went into a jar.

'Is that everything?' Alice asked.

Jeanie checked the recipe and shook her head. 'I'm still missing some vital ingredients.'

Alice's heart sank. 'I *said* it wasn't going to work!'

Jeanie floated over and placed a hand on Alice's shoulder. 'Don't fret, my dear. I said *I* was missing them. Not you. I require a single drop of a shapeshifter's blood.' She looked from Alice to Louis. 'Which of you young werewolves would like to volunteer?'

Both Louis and Alice shot a hand out towards the genie. Then Alice pulled hers back. 'Better use Louis's blood,' she said. 'In case I'm really not a werewolf any more.'

Jeanie took a needle from her bench, held it over a flame for a second, then gently pressed it into Louis's finger. A drop of blood squeezed out. Jeanie caught it in a test tube.

After glancing at the recipe again, she said, 'As well as revealing the Karamorph's real form, we must hide that which she has stolen. Who has the ability to hide from prying eyes?'

Everyone looked under the bench at Dustin, who was deeply engrossed in the *Kronikel*. He shook his head as he puzzled over a passage of text, sending a cloud of brownie dust into the air. Jeanie quickly caught some of the dust, and stirred it into the test tube.

'Finally,' she said, 'I need a cat's whisker.' She

reached out and plucked one from Miss Pinky's cheek.

'Ouch! Did you have to do that?' cried Miss Pinky, rubbing her cheek.

Jeanie laughed. 'Actually, no. But I didn't want you to feel left out.' She dropped the white whisker into an empty tube. 'Although it might come in useful one day.'

Jeanie added Alice's blood and Dustin's dust to the jar and then set it over a flame, where it immediately began to bubble and smoke. 'Here goes,' she said, ducking under the bench. Then she peeped out. 'You should probably all do the same.'

Alice and Louis scrambled in next to Dustin, while Miss Pinky screamed and cat-leaped over the bench to join them. Wedged up against Louis, Alice could feel his heart thumping. Hers was beating just as fast. *Please work, please work*, she thought.

BANG!

The bench shuddered and dense brown smoke

billowed in the air. The smoke filled Alice's lungs. Judging by everyone else's reactions, it smelled as toxic as it looked.

'Masks might have been an idea,' said Miss Pinky though her hands.

Louis fanned himself frantically. 'That smells worse than a rotten cockatrice egg.'

As soon as the air had cleared a bit, they all climbed out. Alice was relieved that the glass jar hadn't broken. Instead, a thick-looking blue liquid floated on the top, with a layer of bright pink smoke rolling around underneath it.

'Is it supposed to look like that?' asked Alice, peering into the jar.

Jeanie consulted the recipe. 'It doesn't say.'

'So there's no way of knowing if this stuff's going to work,' said Miss Pinky. 'It'll be just like the time I made my own dye for my paws.'

'What happened?' asked Alice.

Miss Pinky laughed. 'The fur all fell off, so I suppose you could say it *died*! Took months to grow back.'

'I'm afraid you are just going to have to take it to these awards and try your luck,' said Jeanie.

Alice gave Jeanie a hug, which was an odd experience. It was a bit like trying to hug Fergus Fingal. There was nothing solid to hold on to.

'We should go,' said Louis. 'Look at the time!'

'The Nessies!' cried Alice. 'The ceremony will be starting soon. How far is the venue from here?'

Miss Pinky grimaced. 'It's way up the coast. The location has to be remote because they don't want random humans turning up.'

In all the talk about runes and serums and shapeshifters, nobody had thought about how they were actually going to get to the Nessies. Alice turned back to Jeanie. 'Don't suppose you've got a griffin anywhere, have you?' she said.

'Afraid not,' said the genie. 'What you need is a wyrm.'

'A worm?'

'No, a wyrm.'

Alice pulled a face. 'That's what I said.'

'You said worm with an "o", while I said wyrm with a "y",' Jeanie explained. 'There's a difference.'

'How can this wyrm-with-a-y help us?' asked Louis.

'Wyrms can cover massive distances in no time at all,' said Jeanie. 'They travel through a network of tunnels.'

'Like the London underground?' said Alice.

Jeanie stared at her, confused. 'No, like wyrms.'

Miss Pinky scratched her head. 'I wonder . . .' She tapped away at her phone again. 'Result! There's a wyrm on the Chuber app.' She dropped her phone into her pocket. 'Booked it.'

'How long until it arrives?' asked Alice.

'They're usually pretty speedy,' said Miss Pinky.

'*Très bien*,' said Louis. 'Because my ears have detected a problem and it's heading this way.'

A deafening alarm began to sound, making test tubes and bottles vibrate off shelves across the lab. Alice lunged for the serum just as it was about to crash to the floor.

'Attention! Attention! Lockdown procedure initiated! MonLab is now on maximum alert!'

'It's the vampires!' Alice screamed. 'They've sniffed me out!'

13. WYRM HOLE

'Incoming!' screamed Jeanie. In a puff of green smoke that would have been very effective as a theatre special effect, she vanished into her elderflower cordial bottle.

The floor shook. Glass jars rattled and the serum slopped around inside its container. Louis grabbed Jeanie's bottle before it could fall off the workbench and smash.

Suddenly the entire back wall exploded. Bricks went flying, and what Alice could only describe as a massive grey sausage burst out of the gaping hole. It stopped centimetres from where she stood caked in a layer of rubble and brownie dust. The end of the sausage opened, revealing a revolving circle of teeth sharp enough to slice through stone.

'Wyrm for Pinky,' it said, then let out a knee-shaking belch. 'Where to, love?'

Flicking bits of debris off her T-shirt, Miss Pinky rushed forward. 'Impressively speedy service,' she said. 'Five stars. Would highly recommend.'

Peering through the dust-filled air, Alice saw the lift doors open. A posse of purple-cloaked MIA vampires dashed out. 'Suspect spotted!' screamed one.

Another sniffed the air, her nostrils flaring. 'Blood verified.'

'Stop in the name of Monster law!' boomed the first vampire, swooping past the lab benches. Technicians ducked for cover or flew up to the ceiling.

'We need to go,' said Alice firmly. 'Now!'

She shoved the jar of serum in her satchel and ran towards the wyrm. Bristly hairs encircled its dark purple

lips, while here and there, even thicker hairs poked through its elephant-like skin. There was a light strapped to its head. It belched again, blowing Alice's hair up around her face.

'Ever tried flossing?' asked Miss Pinky, wafting her hand in front of her nose.

She grabbed one of the thicker hairs and pulled herself on top of the wyrm. 'What are you waiting for guys?' she yelled.

'Stop that wyrm!' shouted another vampire. 'Our fangs are filed and we're hungry for blood!' Louis clambered up next. Alice was about to join him when she remembered Dustin.

Scanning the area, she spotted one of his pink toes poking out from under a piece of plaster. She heaved the plaster off, pulled the brownie to his feet and pushed him towards the wyrm. Dustin stumbled dizzily, still clutching the dictionary to his chest, dangerously close to the monster's revolving teeth.

'*Allez-oup*,' said Louis, reaching for Dustin and pulling him on to the wyrm's back.

Alice grabbed a bristly wyrm hair and pulled herself up, wedging in between Louis and Dustin.

'Where's Jeanie?' she shouted as the wyrm began to heave itself back through the hole. She knew the vampires would arrest the monster chemist for helping them get away.

'Here!' Louis, waving the green mist-filled bottle he had rescued.

Alice slipped the bottle into her satchel beside the serum. She ducked to avoid a falling piece of brick.

'Hold tight,' called the wrym.

It pulled out of MonLab seconds before the MIA officers reached them. Alice's last glimpse of the lab was the vampires' fangs, gnashing in frustration. There was no stopping now until they reached the Nessies, because the MIA would be hot on their heels. Or rather, hot on the wyrm's tail.

As the wrym sped along, Alice clutched her satchel tight. Beneath her, pulses of energy rolled in waves along the wyrm's body. Talking was impossible due to the din from the rush of air, so Alice had to shout to be heard. 'How do wyrms actually move?' she yelled to Miss Pinky.

'Who cares!' Miss Pinky shouted. 'Their slogan

is, "From A to Z as quick as can be". That's all that matters!'

Alice concentrated on holding on tight as they veered around bends in the tunnel. On one especially sharp bend, Dustin almost slipped off. If it hadn't been for Alice grabbing a handful of his hair, the brownie and his dictionary would have been crushed under a thousand tons of fast-moving wyrm blubber. Alice quickly tied some of Dustin's hair around her waist as an emergency seat belt.

Thankfully, the rest of the ride was incident free. Alice had just mastered how to balance her weight when the wyrm decided to put on the brakes. Everyone was thrown forward as the creature skidded to a bone-shaking halt.

Louis screamed as he crashed into Alice. Alice in turn smashed into Dustin.

'Pile up!' screamed Miss Pinky as Alice heard the

unmistakable crunch of breaking glass from inside her satchel.

'You have reached your destination,' the wrym said, belching out a cloud of earth.

'You need to work on your braking technique,' said Miss Pinky.

They all slid off the wyrm. Alice completely forgot that Dustin's hair was still tied around her waist, so they slid off together into a heap. There was the sound of more crunching glass.

Alice anxiously pulled her satchel open. In the dim light cast by the wyrm's head lamp, she could see a pale mist rising up from the glittering shards in the bottom of the bag. The serum! Horrified, Alice watched it spiral up in front of her. In a moment it would be lost for ever in the tunnel.

But then, to her relief, the mist twisted into something more solid. Something more human-looking.

'Whoa!' said Jeanie. 'That was quite a ride!'

Alice could hardly bear to look inside her satchel again. When she did, all she could see was a ball of tissues in the corner. She looked at Jeanie. 'Is the serum OK?'

Jeanie peered into the satchel. 'It's fine. All those used tissues in your bag protected it.'

'Ew,' said Louis.

Alice carefully lifted the jar out, pulling away the manky tissues. The serum was safe. But Jeanie's bottle was destroyed.

'I'm sorry Jeanie,' said Alice, shaking out her satchel. The remains of the genie's home sprinkled to the ground.

'Don't worry,' said Jeanie. 'I've been thinking about moving for a while. I could use a bit more space.'

They thanked the wyrm and made their way up a steep slope cut into the tunnel wall, emerging into the late afternoon sunlight. The ocean sparkled nearby, and towering cliffs loomed above a beach thronging with monsters of all shapes and sizes and species.

'Wowser!' gasped Miss Pinky.

Alice spun round. *Wowser* summed up the view pretty accurately. Camera flashes lit up the darkening sky, and twinkled off the sequinned gowns and suits of the monsters as they sashayed along a red carpet towards a huge cave cut into the rocky cliff face. Waves from the ocean lapped right up to another opening just along from the red carpet. Alice was certain she saw a couple of flapping mermaid tails disappearing through the entrance.

I'm here, thought Alice. *I'm really at the Nessies.*

14. DRESS TO IMPRESS

They had arrived at the location for the Nessies in one piece, apart from Jeanie's bottle. But that didn't mean getting in to the awards was going to be simple. In fact, the next stage of the mission was going to be even more tricky.

Miss Pinky led everyone behind a large rock in the sand. Peering around the side, Alice had a clear view of the cave entrance. A crowd of monsters had gathered under a fancy canopy at the end of the red carpet, with a long queue of yet more creatures clamouring to get in. Most were arriving by air. Alice spotted a patch of sand nearby where all manner of flying creatures were landing, including several griffins and a giant cockerel with dragon wings.

'You don't see many cockatrices these days,' said Miss Pinky, peeking over Alice's shoulder. 'They're one of the rarer types of MOMs on the Ministry database.'

Alice scanned the crowd for a glimpse of the Karamorph, but guessed the star of the show was already inside.

'Shouldn't we be over there with *tout le monde*, and not *ici* behind this rock?' asked Louis.

'The boy's right,' said Dustin, staring at the spectacle through his parted fringe. 'I don't care for nonsense like this, but we ought to get moving.'

'*Nonsense!*' shrieked Miss Pinky. 'This is not nonsense. This, my hairy friend, is a once-in-a-lifetime glamourtunity!'

'But we can't just rock up with all the other guests,' Alice pointed out. 'There's bound to be a security check, and me and Louis are wanted by the MIA.' A piece of paper fluttered down at her feet. She picked it up, read it, and handed it to Louis. 'See? Another wanted flyer,' she said.

Louis pulled a face. 'They've made us look like real criminals this time.'

Miss Pinky grabbed it and purred angrily. 'They've photoshopped MonsterMax prison boiler suits on to you both! And let me tell you, whoever said orange is the new black did not have ginger hair.'

'And they've increased the reward for information,' said Dustin, reading off another flyer as it flew past on a sudden breeze. 'Now they're offering a private audience with Kiki on top of the cash.'

'Idiots.' Alice shook her head. 'The Karamorph will eat them alive.'

'To be fair, half her fans would probably be happy to die just to get that close to her,' said Miss Pinky,

'Or rather, close to Kiki.'

Alice spotted a couple of young elves taking a selfie in front of the red carpet. They were wearing identical T-shirts emblazoned with the words *Freaki for Kiki* in rainbow letters. Alice reckoned they'd gladly hand her and Louis over to the MIA in exchange for meeting the host of the Nessies.

'We need to disguise ourselves fast,' she said. 'Any ideas?'

Everyone looked around, as if a treasure chest of cunning disguises was going to suddenly appear on the beach. But sometimes, as Alice had learned on her recent mission to rescue the royal cyclops, the solution to solving your problem wasn't always obvious. Sometimes you had to think outside the box.

'Look!' she said, pointing to the canopy. 'We could use some of that material to make a disguise. We just need to get over there without being spotted.'

Jeanie cleared her throat. 'Perhaps I can be of assistance,' she said. 'How about I create some fog? Just enough to give you some cover.'

'Can you do that?' asked Alice.

'I'm a genie,' said Jeanie, winking. 'Your wish is my command.'

She closed her eyes and began to dissolve into a fine grey mist, which thickened rapidly into a column of fog just wide enough to hide them all. The fog drifted slowly across the beach towards the canopy. If anyone was surprised to see a random patch of fog, they quickly lost interest. There were far more exciting things happening on the red carpet.

When they reached the canopy, Miss Pinky unhooked one of the purple curtains. It would have looked very odd to any of the monsters if they'd been able to see. Luckily, Jeanie's mist was thick enough to shield the whole thing.

'It's velvet,' whispered Miss Pinky, rearranging the rest of the curtains so there was no visible gap.

Still cloaked in Jeanie's fog, they moved away a short distance. Dustin plonked himself down and opened the rune dictionary while Miss Pinky held up the velvet curtain.

'What do you think?' asked Alice. 'Can you do something with it?'

Miss Pinky's eyes gleamed. 'You bet,' she said,

kicking off a boot and extending her cat's claws. 'Time to get creative!'

After just a few minutes of ripping and shredding, knotting and twisting, she held out a pile of purple velvet to Alice. 'Ta da! We can wear these like saris or Roman togas.'

'We?' said Alice.

Miss Pinky rolled her eyes. 'Like . . . duh! I'm not going to the ceremony dressed like a sad wannabe. Especially not with you looking a gazillion dollars in this fabulous frock.'

She helped Alice to wind the velvet around herself. Then Alice did the same for Miss Pinky. Next, Miss Pinky twisted two smaller pieces of the velvet into elaborate head-dresses, which reminded Alice of Medusa's snake-covering turban. It was such a shame Medusa and Polyphemus weren't here. Having two ultra-powerful monsters like a gorgon and a cyclops on their side would have been really useful against whatever they were going to face inside the cave.

'What about *moi*?' asked Louis. 'I still look like Louis Loup-Garou, wanted for crimes against meat eaters!'

Miss Pinky frowned. 'I don't have any more velvet left.'

'Fashion is the least of our concerns,' said Dustin, head still buried in the pages of the dictionary. 'The more of these runes I understand, the worse this Karamorph sounds. If Kiki really is this shapeshifter, we need to lock her up as soon as we can.'

Alice stared at Dustin, sitting in the sand with his long hair spread all around him. *I wonder . . .* she thought.

'Louis,' she said. 'Do you reckon you can carry Dustin on your shoulders?'

'*Quoi*?' asked Louis, looking a bit startled.

'Huh?' asked Dustin, looking up from the dictionary.

Alice helped Dustin to his feet. 'Your hair's long enough to cover Louis's face, at least,' she said. 'Let's try it out.'

Louis knelt down in front of the brownie, who clambered on to his shoulders still clutching the enormous dictionary. Alice and Miss Pinky quickly rearranged Dustin's hair, which reached below Louis's neck.

Alice clapped. 'It's brilliant!'

'Yay!' Miss Pinky skipped on the spot. 'We've created a brand new MOM! A werebrownie!'

'*Mon Dieu!*' Louis puffed from somewhere under the hair. 'With this dictionary, Dustin is *très* heavy!'

'OK,' said Alice, checking her turban for stability. 'Let's go!'

Miss Pinky sprang over to her with a pencil in her hand. 'One last addition,' she said, drawing on Alice's face. 'There!' She quickly took a photo with her phone

and showed it to Alice.

'Whiskers!' Alice shook her head. 'Why?'

'Now you're doubly disguised,' Miss Pinky squealed. 'We look purrfect!' She spun around, then made Alice do the same. 'And tonight's category is . . . monster *eleganza extravaganza!*'

The fog dissolved and Jeanie reappeared. 'You all look fabulous,' she said, as they stepped – or staggered, in Louis's case – towards the cave entrance. 'Good luck!'

The genie remained in human form long enough to accompany them to the cave mouth. Then she transformed again into a fine blue mist and floated up and away over the crowds. Alice felt a brief stab of jealousy. There was no way it was going to be that easy for the rest of them to get into the Nessies.

Seconds later, she was proved right.

15. SECURITY →
CLEARANCE LEVEL YIKES!

They slipped into the queue behind a handsome centaur with long blond hair on his human head and an even longer, blonder tail. He was wearing a smart tuxedo, and his horsehair coat shone as if it had been brushed for hours. Behind them were a couple of giants eating what looked like pebbles from an enormous sack. As they ground the rocks between their teeth, bits of gravel flew out of their mouths, raining down on everyone.

'Watch it!' complained Miss Pinky. 'I haven't got all glamourpussed-up for nothing.' She shook her head. 'Stone giants! No etiquette.'

Suddenly, the line stopped moving. Alice couldn't see past the centaur's body, but Miss Pinky jumped a couple of times, springing high into the air off her paws.

'Uh-oh!' she said, pulling at her whiskers nervously. 'This is not good.'

'What is it?'

'They're using a Hex-Ray,' said Miss Pinky.

'Might as well go home,' grumbled Dustin, holding his twiggy arms out for balance as Louis wobbled dangerously from side to side underneath him.

'*Oui*,' came Louis's muffled voice from under Dustin's hair. 'This could be *un problème*.'

'Is someone going to tell me what this Hex-Ray thing is?' asked Alice.

Miss Pinky sighed. 'She's the most powerful witch in existence, with bionic all-seeing eyes. We don't stand a chance. We'll never get past her. It's goodbye Nessies, hello MonsterMax.'

The centaur trotted on a few steps and Alice saw the Hex-Ray witch. She was a tall, blue-cloaked figure with long, straight, grey hair. Her face was already creepy enough with its pointed chin and wide, toothless mouth, but it was made even more horrid by the huge gaping holes where her eyes ought to have been. These, it turned out, were being

held in the witch's hands like giant ping-pong balls, and she was using them to scan every monster who walked past.

Alice watched as the Hex-Ray scanned the centaur. He was obviously really nervous because he deposited a pile of manure as he was being scanned. *These centaurs really need to learn some toilet manners*, she thought.

The gruesome witch waved her eyes around the centaur and instantly began screeching wildly. 'Beep! Beep! Beep!' she wailed. 'Security breach!' Her hands flew up to her face and she shoved both eyes back into their sockets, where they spun around until facing the right way. Then she plunged her fingers into the centaur's tuxedo pocket, removed a camera and flung it to the ground, where she stamped it to dust with a calloused heel.

'No filming and no photography,' she snarled.

The centaur trotted away, grumbling. Alice slowly

stepped forward. She didn't have a phone or camera, but she was carrying some very important serum in her satchel. She looked up at the Hex-Ray, wondering if a smile would help. But the witch merely blinked a couple of times, and then popped her eyes back out.

'Your turn!' snapped the Hex-Ray, pointing a green eye at her.

Alice took a huge breath and stood as still as her quivering knees would let her. The witch scanned her up and down with an eye on either side. She held her eyes in front of Alice's face for ages.

Oh no! She isn't fooled by my whiskers, thought Alice, hardly daring to breathe.

'What are you?' snapped the Hex-Ray.

'I'm . . . er . . . a MOM,' stammered Alice.

'She's my sister,' said Miss Pinky.

Alice nodded. 'Meow!' she said.

The eyes blinked, then the witch passed them over

Alice's satchel. 'What's in the bag?' she cackled.

'It's my . . . um . . . medicine,' said Alice, mind working overtime. 'To stop me coughing up hairballs.'

'Hairballs?' The Hex-Ray whipped an eye back in front of Alice's face. If it could detect a lie as big as the one she'd just told, she was for it!

'Yes,' said Alice. She held her hand over her mouth and coughed. 'I think I can feel one coming up—'

The Hex-Ray poked out its long grey tongue. 'Revolting creature! Move on!'

Alice, stunned by the success of her play-acting, walked away as calmly as possible. The Hex-Ray had only just started on Miss Pinky when the witch began screeching again.

'Beep! Beep! Beep! Security breach! Telephone detected! Hand it over now!'

Miss Pinky looked horrified as she pulled her beloved phone from her velvet robes. The Hex-Ray took it and threw it to the ground, stamping it to pieces as she'd done with the centaur's camera.

'You've crushed it!' Miss Pinky wailed.

'No phones allowed,' said the Hex-Ray.

'So not fair,' mumbled Miss Pinky, joining Alice. 'Every time we're on a mission, my phone gets destroyed.'

They watched as Louis staggered forward. Dustin teetered on his shoulders, just managing to hold himself upright.

'She'll see under the hair,' whispered Alice, as the Hex-Ray began scanning Dustin from the top of his head. But just as the eyes passed down his body, he shot his little hand out and a small cloud of brownie dust puffed over the witch's eyes. The Hex-Ray staggered back and began furiously licking her eyeballs and screaming about the sand and wind and having to work in difficult conditions. Louis and

Dustin quickly tottered past.

'We did it!' said Alice, as she and Miss Pinky helped Dustin down. 'We're all in!'

They followed the red carpet through a crevasse in the rock and into the cave itself. As they rounded a corner, Alice was dazzled by a sparkly brightness. Looking up, she found the source. Literally thousands of sprites flittered around, casting their stunning light beams like lasers around the quartz-studded rocks. If Aladdin's cave had been real, it would have looked just like this, decided Alice.

But if that was spectacular, what they saw as they continued deeper inside the cave was beyond amazing. Two lines of dragons either side of the path formed a guard of honour. Their scales flashed in multi-coloured splendour and they breathed jets of fire overhead.

'Now *this* is what I call making an entrance,' said Miss Pinky, eyes glinting in the flames.

'*C'est incroyable!* It is unbelievable,' said Louis, stretching as Dustin jumped down from his shoulders. His skin glowed in the bright light and his gap-toothed smile seemed to fill his entire face.

'It is,' agreed Alice. But she still felt her heart sinking when she thought about how much fun the

Nessies would have been if she didn't have the whole confront-the-Karamorph-and-try-to-get-her-werewolf-powers-back thing going on.

The long line of dragons finally ended and they found themselves in a vast cavern. A huge pool rippled as a team of synchronised mermaids flipped and dipped, flashing their beautiful tails in time to music.

Miss Pinky cheered. 'It's the Swimtacular Sirens! Monster World champions!'

Alice could have watched the mermaids perform for ages, but her eyes were drawn to the huge stage behind the pool. A waterfall backdrop ran with golden water. More sprites and other winged creatures flew in a circle over the stage, trailing ribbons from the ceiling, while a troop of dancing nymphs leapt and spun across the silver floor.

'Wow,' said Alice. 'Just, wow.'

It was only now that she noticed the tables arranged around the pool. Stone walkways crossed the water, providing routes to the stage for those lucky enough to win a Nessie. Every table hummed with the chatter of excited monsters, squawking and roaring to each other. Griffins ruffled their plumes at one table. At another, centaurs shared a joke. At a third table, a family of vampires raised glass goblets in a toast. The goblets, Alice noticed, were filled with red liquid, which she guessed wasn't tomato juice. Meanwhile, overhead, gold-skinned babies flew around carrying trays of drinks and food.

'Cherubs!' cried Alice.

'They've been spray-painted gold,' said Miss Pinky, ducking as one of the them nearly clanged her on the head with his empty tray.

'Sorry, love!' the cherub called out as his wings flapped to gain height.

'Let's just hope they're all potty-trained,' muttered Miss Pinky. 'Because I didn't bring an umbrella.'

Alice quickly spotted a table which was empty apart from two figures. She smiled. Magnus's orange hair was unmistakable, even from a distance. There might as well have been a giant arrow pointing at him. *Just as well I'm wearing this turban*, thought Alice.

'There they are,' she said, gathering her gown around her ankles. 'Magnus and Doogie.'

She carefully made her way down some steps. Now would not be the time to draw attention to herself by falling over into the water.

16. LIGHTS! CAMERA! TIME FOR ACTION!

'Excuse me. Are these seats taken?'

Magnus' head snapped around so fast, Alice was sure she heard it crack.

'Alice!' He sprang out of his seat and wrapped his niece in a massive hug. 'I hoped you'd find a way to get in. Never doubted it. Not for a moment.'

Alice looked at Doogie, who was smiling broadly too. 'It's true,' he said. 'Your uncle reckoned if anyone could find a way to break into the Nessies while wanted by the MIA, it was you.'

Alice could feel her cheeks blushing bright pink. It was either embarrassment, the heat from the dragons' flames, or both.

'I had some help on the way,' she said. 'These guys have been awesome.'

'You'd better all sit down,' said Magnus. 'Don't want to attract too much attention.'

'Exactly!' exclaimed Miss Pinky, carefully sliding into a seat. 'I don't want to get kicked out now, after all the trouble we've gone to.'

Alice eased herself and her mounds of velvet into a seat, adjusting her head-dress to make sure it was still covering up her hair.

'You both look amazing,' said Doogie. 'Proper award-ceremony chic.'

'So do you,' said Alice, taking in the faun's snazzy waistcoat and knitted tie. One of his horns was pierced and a sparkly ring hung from it. Magnus, meanwhile, had done his best. His tweed jacket had been pressed and his tartan bow tie wasn't even on a piece of elastic.

'Not bad,' Alice added to her uncle, smiling.

'Not bad!' Magnus poked his tongue out at her.

'I was kind of hoping some of Doogie's hipness might have rubbed off on you,' said Alice. 'But I guess it's early days.'

Louis cleared his throat. '*Excusez-moi*,' he said. 'I have seen *ma mère*.' He began to walk away from the table, but Magnus pulled him back.

'I wouldn't if I were you,' he said, in a low, serious voice. 'Your mother is sitting at the Ministry table and you're not supposed to be here, remember?'

'But she will be concerned,' said Louis, looking over to the other side of the vast cave, where Alice could just make out his mum.

'It's OK,' said Magnus. 'I've spoken to her. She knows all about the Karamorph and Alice.'

'And,' said Doogie, 'she knows you're not actual Radical Vegetarian Werewolves.'

'You'll never live that one down,' said Dustin, crawling under the table.

Doogie lifted a corner of the white table cloth. 'What's Dust-Boy doing under there?'

'Research,' said Miss Pinky, checking her reflection in one of the ultra-polished knives.

'He's translating runes,' said Alice, quickly explaining what they'd learnt so far about the Karamorph. 'We think the missing part of the *Kronikel* might give us a better idea of what we're dealing with. Although we don't know if the *serum reveletarium* will really work.'

'So you actually have this serum?' asked Magnus.

'Yes, thanks to Jeanie.' Alice placed the jar on the table. 'Has anyone seen her?'

'I'm here,' came a soft voice from the other side of the table, where an indigo-coloured mist had materialised at an empty place setting. It slowly shimmered into Jeanie's solid form. 'I managed to slip right past the Hex-Ray.'

'How's things at MonLab, Jeanie?' asked Magnus.

'Ah, well,' said Jeanie. 'The research department might be closed for a while for emergency repairs.'

Magnus looked confused, so Miss Pinky explained. 'A wyrm smashed half of it to smithereens.'

'And I smashed Jeanie's bottle,' said Alice. 'So if you find an empty one, let her know.'

'Done!' said Doogie, pouring out some champagne. He placed the empty bottle in front of Jeanie, who smiled.

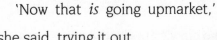

'Now that *is* going upmarket,' she said, trying it out.

A gold-painted cherub flew down with another bottle. 'More fizz,' he shouted in a deep voice. 'Get that down yer gullets.' Then he plonked a bottle of lemonade down too. 'Something for the littluns,' he giggled, before flying off with a burp.

'Charming,' said Louis, pouring out some lemonade for him and Alice.

'Thanks, Louis,' said Alice. She quickly looked around. 'I think you'd better join Dustin under the table. Just in case someone recognises you.'

'Good idea,' said Miss Pinky. 'You can help him with the *Kronikel*.'

Louis shrugged and crawled under the table, banging his head and saying French words Alice thought might not be very polite.

She looked at her uncle. 'This is all very lovely,' she said. 'But is Kiki here?'

Magnus shook his head. 'We haven't seen her at all.'

'It's the Karamorph, not Kiki,' Miss Pinky corrected them. 'And she's here all right. Plus she's brought her charming bodyguards with her. Look.'

Ten manticores had filed on to the stage and taken up position in a semi-circle, their stings raised high behind them. A hush suddenly fell over the cave. The music stopped and the mermaids ceased flipping. The cherubs froze mid-flight. All the monsters in the audience had their eyes fixed on the sprite-lit stage.

A voice boomed out, jingling the glasses and clattering the cutlery on the tables.

'Welcome to the Nessie awards! Please put your flippers, wings, claws and hands together to welcome your host for the evening to the stage. She has more charisma than a charmed chimera. She is as unique as a ukulele-playing unicorn. She has the nerve of a nine-foot knark-swine . . .'

'She's got an ego the size of an Egyptian pyramid,' muttered Magnus.

'Here she is . . . monster vlogging superstar . . . the one . . . the only . . .'

'The absolutely phoney,' whispered Miss Pinky.

'. . . Kiki!'

As the cave erupted in applause and roars, the sprites went wild, flashing like crazy and spinning their spotlights across the cave's vaulted roof until they converged at the top. Then, with a screech that made Alice's ears hum, a creature that was half eagle and half horse soared down over the audience.

'Wow! A hippogryph,' she gasped. 'I've never seen one before.'

It landed with surprising elegance. As it folded its wings back, a figure perched on its saddle dropped gracefully to the stage, shimmering like a mirage in a long silver gown. On her head was the most elaborate

decoration Alice had ever seen: coils of sparkling jewels twined around long turquoise and green feathers which looked like they might have been plucked from a monster-sized peacock.

As the Karamorph strode purposefully across the stage, the troop of manticores flicked their stingers menacingly. But the audience didn't need the threat of a poisonous sting to go wild with applause. They were already on their feet roaring, cheering and squawking.

All except the table from Jobs4Monsters, who sat grim faced, arms firmly crossed.

'She seems taller than last time,' said Alice.

'And this dress she is wearing,' said Louis, peeping out from under the table. 'It is alive, I think.'

'What?' Alice squinted at the Karamorph's shimmering gown. The glistening sparkles everywhere made it hard to see. But then she saw what Louis meant. The dress was made up of hundreds of translucent wings, gently flapping as the Karamorph moved across the stage.

Alice felt like throwing up. The dress was made of real, live fairies.

Next to Alice, Miss Pinky sounded like she was trying to bring up a fur ball, while Magnus and Doogie just sat with their mouths wide open. From inside her new bottle, Jeanie gasped, 'The horror of it!'

Weirdly, no other monsters shared their reaction. Those sitting at the other tables continued cheering and clapping wildly as the Karamorph glided to a glittering golden podium. Shouts of "We love you Kiki!" competed with giants' roars and a chorus of mermaid chanting from the pool.

A young pixie sitting at the next table leaned across to Alice. 'Do you know who designed the dress?' she asked. When Alice shook her head, the pixie looked back at the stage with a dreamy look in her eyes.

'Whoever did it is a total genius. Those wings look incredibly real.'

'They *are* real, you idiot,' muttered Alice under her breath as the manticores whip-cracked their tails to silence the cave.

'Here we go,' said Miss Pinky. 'It's showtime!'

17. AND THE AWARDS GO TO ...

The lights in the cave dimmed and a small group of sprites flittered down to the stage, where they formed a ring just above the Karamorph's head, casting a golden halo of light. The manticores roared at the audience, silencing the laughter and chatter.

Alice gripped the edge of the table. Suddenly, confronting the shapeshifter seemed like the dumbest idea in the world. The audience was whipped up into such a frenzy of adoration that even if she survived, Alice wasn't sure they'd forgive her for spoiling their fun. And even if the serum worked, there was still no guarantee she'd get her werewolf-ness back.

What was I thinking? That I'd simply breeze up there, prove that she stole part of me and ask for it back?

Alice didn't want to think about what would happen if the serum failed. But the words "ripped to shreds" sprang to mind.

'Welcome!' The Karamorph's voice washed over the audience in a wave of sound. Or rather, like multiple waves, because when the Karamorph spoke, it sounded like many voices layered on top of each other. It would have been a brilliant sound effect, if Alice hadn't suspected that they were the voices of the many different monsters the creature had attacked. And that was terrifying.

'Welcome, monsters of fur. Welcome, monsters of feather. Monsters that swim, monsters that crawl, we are all monsters together!'

The audience erupted into yet another frenzy of wild cheering and clapping, apart from Alice's table.

They must have looked like disappointed actors at the Oscars.

'**Monsters short and monsters tall. Monsters who like to slay and maul. Your star is here, hip hip, hooray. It's me! Kiki! And I'm here to stay!**'

The noise from the crowd was immense. Alice checked that the roof wasn't about to cave in with the vibrations caused by the hoof and paw stamping.

The sprites suddenly burst into beams of light, illuminating the Karamorph so that she sparkled centre-stage. Massive screens either side of the stage flashed as she appeared there too, magnified into giant versions of herself. Her ever-changing eyes flipped from blue to grey to red to brown.

'No way!' screamed the silly pixie at the next-door table. 'She's wearing holographic lenses!'

'Like *that's* a thing!' snarled Miss Pinky.

At a nearby table, Alice saw two wrinkly old goblins

faint. A gaggle of young trolls, in fancy pink dresses with plastic wings, screamed and rushed towards the stage over the stone walkways. One of the manticores, who Alice recognised as Barbarus from the press conference, lashed its tail at them, flipping the trolls into the pool.

'That's got to hurt,' whispered Magnus.

'Why aren't they seeing what we're seeing?' asked Alice.

'Because we're the only ones who know,' said Magnus. 'They're all seeing exactly what they want to see: a show with glitz and glamour.'

The Karamorph snapped her fingers and the audience fell into a deep hush. The tension was so thick, Alice would have had to use a chainsaw to cut it.

'Monsters!' said the Karamorph, her voicesuddenly as smooth as one of Doogie's hot chocolate creations. 'My monsters.'

'I'm not her monster!' whispered Alice.

'Friends, followers, fans, we are gathered here this evening in my fabulous presence to honour the biggest, boldest and – I hope – the bravest amongst you,' purred the Karamorph. 'While it is obvious to me, if not to you, that there is only one true Monster of the Year, I have been called on to stand here in all my glory to distribute these charming awards.'

The Karamorph paused while a couple of cherubs flew over carrying a tray loaded with shiny green trophies. She plucked a trophy from the tray and examined it. 'These are modelled on the Loch Ness Monster, you know,' she said. 'I met Nessie once. She's as ugly as a Hook-Nosed Hog Harpie.'

'Hey! I heard that!' called out an old woman towards the back of the cave. Judging from the size of her nose, Alice guessed she was a Hook-Nosed Hog Harpie.

'Now,' said the Karamorph. 'Before I embrace – or

rather, announce – tonight's winners, I expect you are all thinking, who is this sensational superstar you see before you? Where is that dull and dreary Kiki you know from ScreamScreen?'

'That's *exactly* what we want to know,' said Alice, through gritted teeth.

'I know from the thousands of desperate – I mean, adoring – messages I receive daily, that you just can't get enough of Kiki. So I've decided to give you more than you could ever wish for!'

'I don't like where this is going,' said Magnus.

'Let's face it,' continued the Karamorph. 'Vlogging is so yesterday. What's the point in being on your screens where I can't see your delicious faces? Or where I can't taste – I mean, touch – you?'

Alice never wanted to feel the Karamorph's touch again. She pulled a corner of the table cloth up and peered underneath the table. 'Please say you have something for us, guys?'

Dustin and Louis looked up from the rune dictionary, which they were reading by the light of a tiny sprite they'd trapped under an upturned glass vase.

'Almost there,' said Dustin. 'Just a couple more symbols to translate.'

Back on the stage, another cherub fluttered down with a plump fistful of silver envelopes. The Karamorph grabbed the envelopes, and then seized the cherub by its foot for a moment while it wriggled and sobbed. Alice watched in horror as the shapeshifter dropped the cherub on to the floor, where it flopped limply on to its fat little tummy.

'Such a cry-baby,' the Karamorph said, laughing. She clicked her fingers. Barbarus sprang forward, picked the motionless cherub up with his teeth and threw it offstage.

'What did she do to it?' cried Miss Pinky.

'She did exactly what the *Kronikel* says she does,' said Alice grimly. 'She drained away the cherub's life force for herself.'

'That's terrible!' exclaimed Doogie.

'It's what she's got planned for all of us,' said Alice, glaring at the stage.

The Karamorph was preparing to hand out the awards. 'Tonight's first award,' she announced, 'is for this year's Strongest Monster.' She ripped open a silver envelope. 'And the Nessie goes to . . . oh, goody, I've always wanted to eat – I mean, meet – this creature! It's Bernard Blunderbone, the Stone Giant!'

The cave erupted in an explosion of wild applause. A violent vibration nearly toppled Jeanie's champagne bottle as a group of giants at the back of cave pounded the ground with their feet. Alice recognised one of the giants from the red carpet. He thundered towards the stage, sending tables, chairs and smaller monsters flying in all directions as he leaped over the pool in a single bound and thumped across the stage to the Karamorph, who awaited him with outstretched arms.

'Congratulations!' she cried, grabbing him by the hand. The stone giant went completely rigid.

'Poor wee thing's in shock,' the pixie told her friends.

Alice and Miss Pinky exchanged frustrated eye-rolls.

'Poor thing's in her evil grasp more like,' said Magnus. 'And there's nothing "wee" about him!'

The Karamorph held on to the giant for a minute before releasing him. He collapsed with such force that every glass in the cave seemed to rattle.

'Bless him,' said the Karamorph, whose voice had suddenly become much deeper. 'The shock of winning really got to him!' And she summoned the manticores, who hauled him away.

Watching in horror as the lifeless bulk of the stone giant disappeared into the wings, Alice saw that the Karamorph was growing. She'd become taller and her body seemed to bulge inside her gown, pushing against the seams.

'Wow,' squeaked the pixie, bouncing up and down in her seat. 'These special effects are amazing! They've made Kiki seem bigger!'

Alice groaned. All around her, monsters were talking about how fantastic the show was, and how they'd never seen special effects like it before. She peeked back under the table. 'Come on Dustin! She's building to something.'

'Nearly done,' he said, flipping through the dictionary frantically.

Alice gave him a quick thumbs-up. She was desperate to know what the *Kronikel* said, but at the same time, she dreaded it.

'Next up is the Nessie for Fiercest Monster,' boomed the Karamorph. Ripping the envelope open, she threw her head back and laughed. 'Oh good! The Nessie goes to Durmdrach, the Horned High-Back Dragon.'

A heart-stopping roar echoed from the vaulted cave roof and a huge shadow descended over the audience. Durmdrach crashed on to the stage, sending long stalactites raining down like arrows. It briefly turned to face the audience in all its shiny-scaled horror. This dragon was nothing like the ones lining the red carpet. It was much larger, with horns along its massive back. Glittering green scales covered its body and outstretched wings, giving the beast a metallic sheen. It opened its lizard-like mouth and a jet of red flames shot out across the cave.

'Whatever that dragon's been eating, I don't want any,' said Miss Pinky, as a cherub flapped past, trying to blow out its flaming wing. Alice threw a glass of water over it and the cherub flew away, smouldering.

'Come to Kiki,' crooned the Karamorph as the dragon approached. 'I just love a fierce, flying, fiery monster!'

"Don't do it!" shouted Alice.

Nobody heard her over the applause. The Karamorph already had her hands around the dragon's neck. When she let go, the enormous creature flopped to the ground with a loud thump.

'Another monster overcome with emotion.' The Karamorph's voice had a new edge to it. 'I think we'll take a break while we clear him away.'

If Alice's eyes weren't deceiving her, the Karamorph's skin had a green tinge to it now. A click of her fingers brought the manticores skittering forward to pull the dragon's body away,

'That poor dragon,' said Louis, who had poked his face out from under the table and was watching in disbelief.

'If you hadn't pulled me away in time,' said Alice, 'that's what would have happened to me.'

Louis shook his head. 'And all these other monsters . . .' He looked around the cave with despair. 'They think it is entertainment.'

'You're right,' said Alice. 'Nobody seems to care.'

'They *should* care,' said Dustin, emerging from

under the table with his notebook in one small hand and the original *Kronikel* in the other. 'I've finished the translation.'

'And?' asked Alice, immediately knowing she didn't want to hear the answer.

'And she's going to destroy us all,' said Dustin.

18. DRESS TO DISTRESS

There was an uncomfortable silence which lasted for about five seconds, but felt to Alice like five hours. Then Miss Pinky laughed.

'Ha!' she said. 'For a moment I thought you said she's going to destroy us.'

'That's exactly what he did say,' said Alice.

Dustin nodded. 'I couldn't decipher all of the symbols, but I'm fairly certain that they say that the Karamorph will bide her time until she has enough energy and monster power to begin the Day of Doom.'

'The what?!' cried pretty much the whole table.

'The Day of *Doom*,' repeated Dustin, putting extra

emphasis on the 'doom'.

'Stop saying that,' said Miss Pinky with a terrified mew. 'You're making me nervous.'

'You did ask,' said Dustin. 'According to these runes, the Day of Doom is the day a vengeful shapeshifter will wreak terror on the world that has ignored her powers and allowed humans to rule the planet.'

'Crikey,' said Magnus, slumping back into his chair.

'Gosh,' said Doogie.

'Never in all my misty years,' said Jeanie, popping her head out of the champagne bottle.

'Are you sure about this, Dustin?' asked Alice.

Dustin handed her his notebook. 'Read it for yourself. I'm pretty sure I've translated it properly.'

The brownie had been busy. He'd filled page after page with workings out, scribbles and symbols. On the last page, he'd written two more verses of the *Kronikel* in beautiful curling letters.

Her strength will surge, her power grow,
Until the world her scheme will know.
The fierce, the strong, the oh-so brave,
These are the monsters she doth crave.

Unless her true form be revealed,
Our fates will be forever sealed.
The world laid waste — a lifeless tomb;
Her Hour of Wrath and Day of Doom.

Alice had to agree – it did sound a bit end-of-world-ish. And the Karamorph had definitely been targeting the strongest and fiercest monsters to suck out their energy and powers. But that wasn't the part of the *Kronikel* that she was interested in.

'Guys,' she said, standing up. 'That line about her true form being revealed.'

'What about it?' sniffed Miss Pinky, dabbing at the corners of her eyes. 'Sorry, I'm just not ready for a lifeless tomb.'

'*Moi non plus*,' said Louis, joining Alice on his feet. 'Me neither.'

'None of us want that,' said Magnus. 'Go on, Alice.'

Alice re-read the final verse. 'It says: "*Unless* her true form be revealed." But what if we *do* reveal it?'

Everybody looked blankly at her.

'Come on! Think about it!' Alice urged.

'I am thinking,' said Miss Pinky, clasping her head

tightly. 'And it hurts.'

Dustin crawled out from under the table and released the tiny sprite he'd been using as a reading lamp. It danced just above the table for a second, casting a beam of its light on the jar of serum.

Alice grabbed the jar. 'I reckon if we can reveal the Karamorph's true form, then none of this awful stuff will happen. At least, I hope that's what the *Kronikel* means.'

'But the serum might not work!' cried Magnus. 'No offence, Jeanie.'

Floating just above the table as a violet mist, the genie transformed back long enough to say a quick 'None taken' before mistifying herself again and disappearing into her new champagne bottle home.

'And we might be dead in five minutes time!' Alice glared at her uncle. 'Does anyone here want to take that risk?'

'Of course not.' Magnus got up. 'But we can't just walk up to the stage and chuck this over her.'

'*We're* not walking anywhere,' said Alice. '*I* am.'

Magnus tried to grab the jar away from her, but Alice held it tightly.

'What makes you think you should do this on your own?' he asked her.

'Yeah,' said Miss Pinky. 'We're a team.'

'But it was me she stole something from,' Alice pointed out.

'Alice.' Magnus put his arm around her. 'When will you learn? If she stole from you, she stole from all of us.'

Alice looked at everyone, and everyone nodded back at her.

Doogie put an arm around her too. 'Magnus isn't your only family here, you know. We're *all* family. It doesn't matter if we've got horns, paws or werewolf jaws. Or if we've more hair than a wig maker or we live inside a bottle. We are family.'

'Your monster family,' said Miss Pinky, eyes now in full flood.

'Still, I don't fancy our chances of getting up there,' said Magnus, pointing to the manticores who guarded the edge of the stage.

The manticores stabbed the air with their stinging tails and growled at the front row of tables. Alice had to admit that they were a totally terrifying obstacle to the Karamorph, who now strode back on to the podium. Gone was her fairy gown. She'd changed into a long, green and blue dress. As she crossed the stage, the train flowed out behind her like a fish tail.

Wait – it *was* a fish tail. Karamorph was wearing . . .

'Mermaid!' gasped Miss Pinky. 'She's wearing a mermaid tail!'

Other audience members gasped, but in awe and

delight. The pixie was thrilled, chattering on about finding the designer and having a smaller version made for herself.

'Do you like my new frock?' The Karamorph's voice rang out across the cave. 'It's one I flayed – I mean, made – earlier!'

Alice gripped the serum jar even harder. *If only there was a way up there . . .*

'And so we come to my favourite award of the evening,' boomed the Karamorph, 'The Bravest Monster of the Year. Oh! I can't wait to shake *this* monster's hand.'

'I bet she can't,' muttered Miss Pinky.

The Karamorph sliced the envelope open with her tongue, which looked unpleasantly like a snake's. She removed the card and read it, her eyes glittering with malice.

'Well . . . this is exciting,' she said, licking her lips.

'Wanted across the land for crimes against meat eaters, but celebrated here tonight for courage in the face of certain death, the Bravest Monster of Year is . . . Alice MacAlister!'

19. HERO I GO AGAIN

Despite the top-volume cheers, nobody at the Jobs4Monsters table moved. Alice felt like she had when the Karamorph had held her in her magnetic grasp at the press conference – glued to the spot. She'd heard the award announcement, but it didn't make sense. She even looked around to see who was running over the rock walkways to collect their Nessie.

Louis grabbed her wrists. '*Allo*! Alice! *C'est toi*! You have won!'

Alice just stared at him.

'Alice! Go on! This is your chance.'

She shook her head and tried to focus. Louis was

right. It was their only chance.

Alice didn't need to say a thing to Magnus. He already knew.

'We'll be right behind you,' he said. 'Go!'

Alice gulped down some lemonade. Then she swept up her velvet robe and began walking towards the stage.

'Is she here?' said the Karamorph. 'Has Alice MacAlister managed to evade the MIA and sneak her way into the Nessies? I do hope so. I'm simply desperate to embrace this brave, brave creature!'

The shapeshifter's voice thundered into Alice's chest. But instead of turning her legs to jelly, the sound made her feel more solid than ever.

Holding the serum firmly, Alice weaved through the tables. She smiled at a group of banshees wailing 'Congratulations!' at such a high pitch that a couple of champagne glasses shattered. She even high-fived a phoenix's wing as she passed its table. The important thing was to look as innocent as possible. Right until she was face-to-face with the Karamorph.

Crossing the walkway, Alice glanced at the mermaids in the water. She gritted her teeth as she thought about the poor mermaid who'd been turned into the Karamorph's dress.

You've hurt your last monster, she thought as she reached the stage.

'What have we here?' roared the Karamorph.

Alice stopped dead. She hadn't even made it past the manticores yet.

The Karamorph had taken a giant stride across the stage and was piercing Alice with a vile, yellow-eyed glare. 'This is not how I remember you looking.' She blinked, her eyes flashing different colours like disco lights. 'Step closer this instant and remove that ridiculous head-dress!'

Still clutching the serum in one hand, Alice unwound the velvet wrap, dropping it on to the stage.

'So it really is you!' cried the Karamorph. 'Alice MacAlister in all your ginger-haired glory! Why don't you remind us all of the act of bravery you are receiving this lovely, shiny Nessie for?' She held the award up so that it glinted like an emerald in the sprite-light.

'Oh, you know,' said Alice. 'Stopping an evil monster from trying to take over the monster world.' *Just like I am now*, she could have added, but decided she'd better not. Yet.

'I was hoping that the MIA or pathetic human police would have caught you by now,' hissed the Karamorph, leaning in to prevent her voice from being heard by the audience.

'It's you they should be hunting for,' Alice whispered back. 'You're nothing but a thief!'

'Me? Kiki? A thief?'

'Only you're not Kiki, are you?' Alice challenged. 'You're the Karamorph!'

The shapeshifter's eyes flashed through a kaleidoscope of colours from the hundreds of creatures trapped inside her. She let out a horrible cackle that sounded like it came from the very depths of her being. 'There's no Nessie for being a smartypants,' she snapped.

So, we got that much right at least, Alice thought. *She is the Karamorph.* She tried not to look at the mermaid-skin dress. She was pretty sure she recognised the scales from the fish-gilled reporter at the press conference.

'And you *are* a thief!' Alice said, shivering as the Karamorph's reptile tongue flickered in and out. 'You stole my smellability and I want it back!'

'I'll be taking more than that in just a moment,' snarled the shapeshifter. 'I'll finish the job that gap-toothed boy interrupted, and drain every last drop of your bravery.'

'No, you won't,' said Alice. 'You've taken enough lives already.'

The Karamorph pouted and batted her eyelids. 'Oh, go on! Just one more. It's why I absorbed Kiki and took this awards gig in the first place. To meet all these fabulous monsters. Draining their life forces has made me more powerful than ever!'

'You reckon?'

Alice couldn't believe what she was about to do. *But I am here for the Bravest Monster award*, she thought. Her fingers shook as she unscrewed the jar. *And doing this is about as brave as it's ever going to get!*

'You should have waited until now to try and steal my bravery,' she said aloud, gripping the jar tightly in case it slipped through her sweaty fingers. 'But you got greedy at the press conference, didn't you?'

A brief flash of worry passed over the Karamorph's face.

Alice knew this was the moment. She didn't hesitate. She threw some serum at the Karamorph and hit her right in the face.

The Karamorph seemed shocked for a moment, then she smiled. The smile twisted into a grimace. Something was brewing inside her.

Something bad.

'How dare you!' she roared. 'Guards!'

Alice was lifted off her feet as one of the manticores raised her into the air. But hanging from the tip of a scorpion's sting was possibly safer than remaining on the stage next to the Karamorph.

Down there, it looked like the shapeshifter was on the verge of a catastrophic explosion. Kiki's beautiful face had turned a sickening shade of deep purple.

Her hands and fingers were expanding like a clown's balloons into grotesque, five-legged creations. And her eyes weren't just bloodshot. They were actually bleeding.

Alice watched in horror as the Karamorph changed. First into a massive dragon, webbed wings flapping wildly behind it. After a moment, the dragon's face contorted in pain as it morphed into a stone giant.

Then began a series of rapid changes. Every few seconds a new creature appeared as the Karamorph transformed from giant to cherub to lace-winged fairy. For the briefest of moments, Alice saw a fish-scaled merman. The reporter from the press conference! He must have been attacked too. And then Alice saw herself, before the transformations continued.

The formula was working! The Karamorph was revealing every poor monster and human and animal she had ever drained of life and power. With each dreadful mutation came a terrible cry or scream or toe-curling roar.

Alice was vaguely aware of a commotion in the audience. The other monsters were probably fleeing the cave, scared for their safety. She didn't blame them. If she hadn't been hanging from the tail of a poisonous manticore, she'd have been tempted to escape too.

Then she spotted something else. The same creature kept appearing in the fast-changing line-up of the Karamorph's many victims. It wasn't something she'd ever seen in her copy of the *OMG*, or on the monsternet. She doubted even the Ministry had ever classified this appalling thing.

Like a human, it stood upright on long legs. But that was where the similarities ended. A long, forked red tail whipped around behind a gnarled back. Claw-like fingers with long grey nails groped the air while a green tongue licked its face, leaving a film of slime in its wake.

And its face! If a chicken and a lizard and a troll had their faces Photoshopped together, you might come up with something as warty and ugly as this. It was a monster mash of pure evil. If Alice had been standing, there was every chance her legs would have jellified by now.

The Karamorph's transformations were slowing. As they did, the horrible creature seemed to become larger. Its bright yellow eyes grew to the size of tennis balls. Its bony legs bent at the knees.

The Karamorph was preparing to pounce.

The *Kronikel* had got it wrong. They'd made a catastrophic miscalculation. This revolting and deadly-looking creature was the Karamorph's true form – but the serum had made her stronger!

20. TEAM MONSTER

As Alice swung from the giant manticore's scorpion tail, she realised two things. One: she had to try and stop the Karamorph from getting away. And two: she had the solution in her hand. Carefully, she unscrewed the jar again, dipped in her fingers and sprinkled some of the serum over her head.

'Alice! What are you doing?'

Alice looked down. Magnus and Louis were on the stage, ducking and diving as manticore tails lashed at them.

'Hey, Louis!' Alice called down. 'You still desperate to know what it's like to transform?'

'*Bien sûr!*' he cried. 'Of course!'

'Catch!'

Louis caught the jar and wasted no time in sprinkling himself with the serum.

'It's too dangerous!' yelled Magnus, throwing himself flat on his stomach to avoid being stung by a tail.

'Too late!' yelled back Alice. 'And we need some monster power here.'

'Here, Magnus!' cried Louis, lobbing the jar. 'There is some left for you!'

Alice watched her uncle breathe deeply, catch the jar and fumble with the lid. He nearly dropped it, but managed to shake the remaining serum over himself.

For what seemed like ages, Alice was convinced the serum hadn't worked.

Then a surge coursed through every vein in her body. She felt a rush of bubbles pump around her like shaken-up cola, all the way to the tips of her fingers. Her toes tingled, first cold, then warm, then nuclear hot. Alice had the odd sensation that something was pulling at her nails. She tried to focus on her hands, but her vision had blurred.

As she forced a croak out of her mouth, Alice heard the manticore roar and felt herself falling. Somehow, she landed perfectly on all fours. Waves of pain raced along her spine into her legs and arms as she transformed. She heard her bones creak and crack as they expanded. She tasted blood as new teeth forced themselves through her gums.

Alice blinked. Her vision was back. But it wasn't just back. It was *amazing*! Her hands were now sharp-clawed paws. Every ginger hair was visible to her in super-fine detail.

A low snarl made Alice look up.

The Karamorph had also dropped to all fours.

Her tongue flicked across her eyes and hot breath steamed out of her beaked nose.

Alice instinctively pushed her long snout into the air and sniffed her enemy.

A foul, decaying reek filled her nose. The Karamorph's odour was quite possibly the most revolting stench ever created. It was like a toilet block on the last day of a rock festival, mixed with mouldy school-dinner cabbage. But Alice had never been happier.

She could smell again!

Scents filled her head: salty sea, champagne, a hundred different perfumes, the coffee and muffin aroma that followed Doogie everywhere. She made out the sweet smell of elderflower and a musty, dusty odour, which could only be Dustin. They all hit her at the same time, yet she was able to single them out without trying or thinking about it.

Alice's smellability wasn't just back. It was better

than ever.

"ARRROOOOOOOO!"

she howled.

Above the din, two more werewolves howled back.

Alice dug her claws into the stage. The Karamorph did the same. They paced around in a circle, keeping the same distance, snarling and baring their teeth. As they matched each other, step for step, Alice heard a thud next to her. Out of the corner of her eye she saw a dark-haired wolf. Alice recognised Louis's bouncing coils of hair and flame-flecked eyes. He even had a gap between his massive wolf's teeth.

As she and Louis edged closer to the Karamorph, leaping aside every time her scaly red tail whiplashed towards them, a red-furred werewolf landed on the stage. Magnus winked at her with a glacier-blue eye. Alice winked back.

There's no going back now, she thought.

Together, the three werewolves had Karamorph trapped. They encircled her, jaws gnashing and snouts snorting. But then the shapeshifter lunged at Magnus, slicing into his left leg with one of her knife-sharp grey claws. As he yelped with pain and the metallic tang of his blood reached her snout, Alice launched herself at the Karamorph, landing on her arched, knobbly spine and digging her own claws deep into the monster's flesh.

No-one hurts my uncle and gets away with it! yelled Alice, although it came out as a piercing howl.

The Karamorph spun around, thrashing violently, sending Alice flying back onto the stage, The beaky-mouthed monster loomed, taller than ever. Flames shot out of the Karamorph's nostrils as its tail lashed and its claws slashed, slicing deep into one of Alice's back legs.

An ear-shredding cry from the Karamorph's beak brought stalactites crashing down from the cave roof. From either side of her protruding spine, black leathery wings broke through the skin, flapped once and then opened to full stretch.

All three werewolves now attacked the enormous monster together. Louis and Magnus landed on a leg each. Ignoring the blood dripping from her own wound, Alice leapt on to the Karamorph's forked tail, nailing it to the stage with her claws. Their combined weight almost kept the Karamorph grounded, but Alice could feel the creature slowly rising up.

Just when Alice thought they'd lose the battle, the air misted up. A thick rainbow-coloured cloud blinded the Karamorph's beaked head, and a dust bomb exploded. As Alice coughed, she saw a squat, hairy creature tumble across the stage. The Karamorph spluttered and struggled. Alice's leg was hurting badly now, and she wasn't sure how long she'd be able to hold on.

Then, out of nowhere, Miss Pinky leapt at the Karamorph, her paws outstretched and claws glinting sharply. **"YA! KERPOW!"** she screamed, landing a kick on one side of the shapeshifter, before turning and aiming another karate chop on the other side.

The Karamorph howled with rage. With one massive surge of power, she shook the three werewolves from her body. Alice landed on her back with a painful thud, but sprang back to her paws as the shapeshifter prepared to fly again.

Alice didn't think. She simply leapt. Her claws dug into the Karamorph's scaly flesh, forcing the creature off-balance. Panting and snarling, Alice clung on, daring the Karamorph to escape.

The shapeshifter was weakening. Her wings beat

more slowly and fire had stopped jetting from her beak. She slumped to the stage. Alice stayed in position for a moment, then looked into Magnus' blue eyes. He nodded, and Alice jumped off her prey.

Before them lay the Karamorph. Puffs of smoke oozed from her beak. The tips of her wings flapped weakly. And then she was still.

'We've done it!' growled Alice.

She poked warily at the grey mound on the stage with her muzzle. The Karamorph began to shrink and change shape yet again. In a matter of seconds, the creature had reduced to a small ball of fur with tiny feet and a long pink tail. It squeaked and scurried around in a circle, jumping to avoid the werewolves' paws.

Just when Alice thought it wouldn't shrink any further, the fur ball vanished and was replaced by a wriggling pink worm. The worm sprouted grey bristly hairs, coiled itself into a tight spring and bounced up and over Alice's head. Before she could react, it wriggled at speed towards the edge of the stage.

'It's getting away!' howled Alice.

She suddenly caught sight of something bounding across the stage. It snatched up the discarded Nessie, somersaulted through the air, and landed firmly on its two hooves.

Doogie!

Doogie looked at Alice, smiled, and dropped the Nessie on the worm. It landed bang on target, spraying mashed bits of the Karamorph in all directions.

Alice leapt over, picked up the Nessie in her paws and bounded back to the others. She held up the award and raised her snout in the air.

Arrooo! she howled. *We're all the Bravest Monsters!*

"*ARRROOOOOOOO!*"

21. DEAL OR NO DEAL?

Drip, drip, drip. Alice watched as the blood slowly trickled through the tube and into her arm. It was the second time that morning that she'd been hooked up to a bag of freshly-donated blood, and it felt weird.

'You OK there, Louis?'

Alice leaned forward, careful not to pull the tube out of her arm. In the bed next to her, Louis gave her the thumbs-up.

'*Oui!*'

The nurses at Saint Beastly's Hospital for Sick Monsters hadn't wanted to let them share a room at first, but in the end had relaxed the rules. In fact, as soon as they found out about their heroic efforts at the Nessies, the staff couldn't do enough for them. They had also had visits from a whole array of monsticians and Ministry for Monsters scientists. Apparently, they were the first Pre-Ts to have transformed into werewolves without a full moon.

Neither Alice nor Louis remembered much about the hours after the destruction of the Karamorph. They had both been injured in the battle, and had lost a lot of blood. To help them recover, they were being given blood donated by Magnus and Louis's mum. And it was working. Alice thought she might even try walking later on.

The ward door opened. Miss Pinky skipped in, carrying a Nessie in one hand and a plate of muffins in the other. 'Good morning! And how are the weeny werewolves doing?'

'Weeny?' Alice said.

'That's what they're calling you!' Miss Pinky laughed. 'Weeny werewolf wonders. You're all over the monsternet. It's practically all they wanted to talk about in my interview at *Strictly Monstering*.'

'How did it go?' asked Alice, although it was clear from Miss Pinky's huge smile that she'd loved the attention.

'Fab!' Miss Pinky placed the Nessie on the table between the two beds. 'Thanks for letting me take the Nessie into the studio, by the way. It was a real talking point.'

Alice lay back on her pillow. 'It's as much yours as mine, right Louis?'

'Of course,' said Louis. 'I have never seen such *fantastique* karate kicks.'

Miss Pinky beamed, her whiskers twitching and eyes gleaming. 'Thanks guys! Although everyone's saying that you're the real hero, Alice.'

'Me?' said Alice. 'Why? It was a team effort.'

'Yadda, yadda. Blah, blah, blah,' said Miss Pinky. 'You've now defeated two evil monsters who wanted to destroy us all, and you're not even a fully-fledged werewolf yet. Well, apart from the other night, of course. Which, by the way, was totally awesome!'

The door swung open again and one of the nurses trotted in, almost knocking over Alice's blood drip with his centaur's tail.

'Oops,' he said. He checked both patients' bags and turned to Miss Pinky. 'Time to let these two rest.'

Miss Pinky placed the muffins on Alice's bedside table. 'Doogie sends his love. He'll be in later with Magnus.'

Alice breathed in deeply. Doogie's fresh muffins was the smell she was happiest to have back. 'What's Magnus up to this morning?' she asked.

'He's training Dustin back at Jobs4Monsters.'

'Training for what?'

'For his new job, of course,' said Miss Pinky. 'He's been promoted to Research Executive. He won't be doing any more cleaning.'

Alice burst out laughing, which almost ripped the tube out again. 'To be honest, he didn't actually do much cleaning when that *was* his job!'

'I know, right?' said Miss Pinky. 'Oh, and your uncle's going to call Balmoral.'

'What for? Medusa's not there.'

'He's going to speak to their Majesties,' explained Miss Pinky. 'They owe us a favour for rescuing the cyclops, so he's asking them to get you taken off the police's wanted list. Then you'll be able to go home when you're feeling better.'

'Yay!' Alice punched the air. 'I'm not a radical vegetarian criminal any more!'

After Miss Pinky had left, Alice dropped off to sleep for an hour or so. When she woke up, Louis was sitting up reading a copy of *Monsters' Daily*.

'Where did that come from?' she asked.

'*Bonjour*, Alice!' Louis said. 'The nurse left it for us.'

Alice sat up. 'Are we in it?'

'On almost every page!' said Louis, smiling. Then his smile disappeared as he turned to the next page.

'What is it?' Alice asked.

Louis put the paper down and looked at Alice sadly. Alice guessed why.

'They found Kiki, didn't they?' she said.

Louis nodded. 'I am so sorry.'

Alice closed her eyes and pictured the Kiki she wanted to remember from her vlog, with her friendly smile, beautiful green eyes and down-to-earth personality. Ever since she'd seen what the Karamorph did to the monsters at the Nessies, Alice had known that the real Kiki couldn't have survived.

'I might start my own vlog,' she said suddenly. 'And carry on Kiki's work. Hey! We both could.'

'What would we talk about?'

Alice shrugged. 'What it's like to turn into a werewolf, I suppose. We've both done it now.'

Louis eased himself out of his bed and sat on the end of Alice's. 'What was it like?' he asked. 'For you?'

Alice closed her eyes again and tried to remember. It had hurt. She remembered that much. Her bones had grown so fast, she'd actually felt them stretching. But it had also been amazing. The burst of energy she'd experienced. The sense of power and strength. The astonishing vision and hearing, just like a real wolf's. And of course, her smellability had come back. She'd felt invincible.

'I loved it,' she said.

'*Moi aussi,*' said Louis. 'It was the best moment of

my whole entire life.'

Alice nodded. It had been. But she knew her first time was also going to be her last time. She would have to take the antidote now.

'You can be a werewolf again, you know,' said Louis, reading her thoughts perfectly.

'Not in this country I can't,' Alice said. 'It's the law. Remember?'

Louis smiled, showing the gap in his teeth. 'Well then, you will just have to visit me in France and we can be *les loups-garous* together. Do we have a deal?'

Alice looked down at the newspaper. Kiki had never had the chance to enjoy being a werewolf. But Alice knew what it was like now. That wonderful surge of blood coursing through her veins, heightening all her senses. And she knew without a doubt that she wanted to feel it again.

'*Oui!*' she said, smiling back. 'Deal!'

Acknowledgements

Werewolf howls of thanks to:

Andrew, who is a fabulous husband and efficient props master, but who goes missing every full moon. I wish I knew why!

My agent Thérèse Coen, who I suspect might be a Belgian werewolf in London.

Kim Geyer, whose wonderful illustrations would bring a smile to the jaws of even the grumpiest of monsters.

Anne Marie Ryan, for helping to tame my monsters on the page and for bravely suggesting which ones to slay.

Namishka Doshi, for shining the light of publicity on my monsters' faces. Ignore their gnashing teeth and slashing claws – they love it really.

Lynne Manning – your design skills are scarily brilliant.

Everyone at Orchard and Hachette Children's who has helped these monsters escape into the world.

My friends at SCBWI Scotland. I suspect several of you might be vampires, but I shan't hold it against you.

And finally, a terrifyingly loud **"ARRROOOOOOOO!"** to clan #becpub.

Because… well… just because.

JUSTIN DAVIES

Like all superheroes, Justin leads a double life. In one, he flies around the world in his job as cabin crew, visiting all the places he found in his atlas as a boy. In his other life, Justin lives with his husband in Scotland and writes books which he hopes will make you laugh. Although he doesn't have super-smellability like Alice, he can sniff out the best bakery anywhere he goes!

WWW.JUSTINDAVIESAUTHOR.COM

KiM GEYER

Kim designed textiles before taking up her drawing
pencil to illustrate well~dressed characters in
children's books. She lives and works in London with
a brood of her very own monsters and a giant
cactus called Benedict.

WWW.KIMGEYER.COM